Southern Rites

Brian Dorsey

Prelude

McCleary Plantation: February 15, 1865

A booming rattle of thunder shook the house as the flash of lightning illuminated the reflection of Becca McCleary's face. Peering into the darkness beyond the window, her breath formed blotches of fog on the glass as trails of rainwater from the torrent ran down the outside of the window. Anxious, she pulled a kerchief from a pocket in her petticoat and wiped away the fog.

"Miss Becca, you 'ought ta git from 'at winda," said Clara Jefferson, one of the McCleary family slaves.

Lightning flashed again, highlighting Becca's soft features and golden blonde hair. Despite her beauty, Becca's face was twisted and her mouth curled in frustration.

"You hush, Clara," she ordered. Becca and Clara had often played together when they were younger and Clara's tendency to forget her place often infuriated Becca now that they were adults. "If any of our boys come by, I'm gonna wish 'em well." She turned away from the window toward Clara. "And if they stop, you and Carson will bring 'em bacon and biscuits."

"But Miss Becca, ain't barely 'nuf for us. An' day ain't gonna stop. Day been skidadalin' from Charleston all day."

Becca raised her hand to Clara. "Clara, I declare … sometimes I just want to slap some sense into you."

Clara stared back, her nose tilted upward in defiance. "You know ya'll can't, Miss Becca. Mrs. Virginia made Mr. Henry promise no more 'a dat before she—"

"You just get the food when I tell you," she huffed.

Another flash of lightning was followed immediately by the rolling boom of thunder that shook Becca to her bones.

As the rattling of the floorboards subsided, the clanging of metal and sloshing of hoofs in the mud outside drew Becca's attention. "Papa! It must be more of our boys headed out from Charleston," she declared, rushing to the window.

"Girl, get away from that window," ordered Henry McCleary. Becca's father stood at the entrance to the parlor. Broken physically by age and mentally by the loss of his wife and son, his hands shook as he struggled to hold an old musket.

"But Papa," she pouted. "It's our boys."

"And damn it, Clara," cursed Henry. "Turn that lamp out. Ain't nobody needin' to look inside."

"Yessa, Mr. Henry," answered Clara, blowing out the kerosene lamp.

"Now you girls move away from there," he ordered again.

Becca ignored her father; if any Confederate troops stopped, she would greet them. "Just because

Charleston fell doesn't mean I have to stop supporting the Cause." Looking through the window again, she saw several dark figures on horseback stop in front of the house.

The glass fogged again as she continued to stare into the darkness. "They're at the gate, Papa," she declared, wiping the window.

Lightning lit up the landscape as if it were daylight.

Becca let out a gasp as she stumbled away from the window, her hands held to her chest. "No! Yankees!"

The sound of footsteps approaching the door sounded like gunshots.

"Get over here!" ordered Henry.

Her heart pounded, threatening to jump out of her chest.

BAM! BAM! BAM! The door jarred.

Chapter One

The sensation of his head falling jerked Mark Patterson awake. Groggy, he grabbed his coffee. "Damn it!" He spit the cold coffee back into his cup before glancing at his cell phone.

"Shit!" Mark haphazardly shoved his laptop and a stack of hand-written notes into his backpack. He then grabbed a worn volume of *The Official Records of the Union and Confederate Armies*, its pages marked with dozens of yellow, red, and green sticky-tabs. As he placed the old book in his bag, a picture fell onto the desk.

He picked it up and examined it. The 19th century photo was of a young girl in her early twenties. She wore an elaborate dress typical of wealthy Southern families before the war. "Beautiful," he whispered as he flipped it over and read the inscription:

Rebecca McCleary, April, 1862

Letting out a slow sigh, he placed the picture back into the book and began to close it. He stopped, running his hand over the picture. "See you tomorrow, Becca."

A knock at the door drew his attention.

Standing in the doorway was Gerald Han, a

fellow doctoral student' "Thought you'd be here," said Gerald.

"Where else would I be?"

"Well, if I were you, I'd be home with that smokin' hot girlfriend of yours."

Mark chuckled. "She's finishing up a paper in the law library, so she won't be home until eleven or twelve, I'm guessing."

"You've got the perfect girlfriend for a PhD candidate," replied Gerald. "A second-year law student is probably busier than you are … at least she can never complain about the hours you put in."

"I wouldn't say never."

"I'd be more worried about her being late … if you know what I mean," joked Gerald, sitting on the edge of Mark's desk.

"Funny," replied Mark dryly. "I would've expected a Fulbright Scholar to be a little more sophisticated."

"And I would've thought the son of a Supreme Court Justice would be doing something better with his life than digging through old books trying to get a PhD in History." Gerald flipped through another volume of the *Official Records* on Mark's desk. "Not really a degree for a future power-broker."

"Well, Woodrow—"

Gerald guffawed. "Please don't throw Woodrow Wilson in my face … and if you mention Newt Gingrich, I'll jump out of that window," he added, pointing toward the open window of the third-floor office.

Gerald was good company, and actually a good historian, but Mark needed to wrap things up. "So, what's drawing you out of the Song Dynasty manuscripts?"

"I stopped by the main office and saw they put your mail in my box again. And since you prefer this cramped office to the library, I figured you'd still be here," said Gerald, reaching into his bag.

"Thanks. What is it, more flyers for historical journals?"

"Looks like you have two letters." Gerald held up one letter. "To Mark Patterson, Maxwell School, Syracuse University from Virginia Center for Civil War Studies." He pulled out the other letter. "From Mrs. Brianna Mackey, 1 McCleary Lane, McCleary, South Carolina."

Mark snatched the letters from Gerald's hands. "Holy shit!"

"Alright then. I take it you've been waiting for these?"

"Definitely," replied Mark, tearing open the first letter.

"Who the hell's Brianna Mackey?"

"She's a descendant of the McCleary family. Her husband died over twenty years ago so she basically runs the family fortune. She ..." He stopped to read the letter aloud:

'I have considered your request and would love to provide you access to our dear Rebecca McCleary's diary as well as the family records. However, I must request that access only be available at our home in order to preserve the wishes of my mother that the diary not leave the confines of the McCleary Plantation."

He began to scan the remainder of the letter. *"As a further courtesy to you, I would like to offer you residence in the McCleary home during your research ... further arrangements and to assure you are properly introduced ... I will have Mr. Carson Jefferson contact you via email to arrange transportation from the airport to McCleary Plantation when you arrive."*

Mark clinched his fist. "Yes! They gave me access to the diary and their family records."

"Access to a diary no one has seen before. That's like the historian's equivalent of a threesome."

Mark looked up at Gerald. "Very sophisticated."

"What? Fulbright Scholars can't like threesomes?"

Mark stared blankly at Gerald.

"Stop staring at me and open the other letter."

"Fine," replied Mark, opening the second letter. "I've got the access. Now if I get this grant money—"

"Grant money? You have Patterson family money and your father's a freakin' Supreme Court Justice. I'm pretty sure he could just write you a check."

Mark paused to unfold the letter and let out a frustrated sigh. "I need to make it on my own as an academic. I know it sounds stupid, but regardless of how much money my family has, I want to go at my job just like every other historian."

"Well, I guess I'm impressed that you want to do that and at the same time jealous that you have the option. If I—"

"Got it!" interrupted Mark, having glanced at the now open letter.

"Congrats. What are you gonna do now?"

Mark grabbed his backpack and threw it over his shoulder. "Try to make it home before Sarah," he said as he walked to the door. Almost at the door he stopped. "Damn it." Spinning around, he ran back to his desk. "There," he said, grabbing a small velvet box.

"What did ya forget?" asked Gerald.

"I'll tell you tomorrow," replied Mark before

hustling out of the room.

***

Mark sat at the small table in the tiny apartment he and Sarah Barkley shared. He stared at the flickering candle in the center and took several deep breaths to calm himself. "You can do this," he said softly, closing his eyes.

The sound of footsteps coming up the stairs caused his heart to pound again.

He took another deep breath when he saw the doorknob begin to move.

In walked Sarah Barkley.

She was tall and athletic, her shoulder-length brunette hair tied in a tight ponytail. She dropped her backpack onto the floor and started speaking before she looked up. "This lawyer shit had better be worth the time. I …" She froze when she saw Mark standing by the candle-lit table.

"I thought we might have a late dinner. Well … a very late dinner," he said with a slight crack in his voice.

"What is this?" asked Sarah. "If I learned anything in the Army this either means really good … or really bad news."

"They gave me access to the diary," replied Mark with a smile. "And all of their family records."

"That's great news," replied Sarah. "Is that what all of this is for?"

Mark fumbled in his pocket for what seemed like an eternity until he felt the soft velvet cover of the container. Gripping the box tightly, he pulled it from his pocket and presented it to Sarah. "I just thought that a plantation in Charleston would be a great place …" He knelt and opened the box. "To celebrate our engagement … that is if you say yes?"

Mark let out a deep sigh of relief when he saw a smile come to her face before she placed her hands to her mouth. "… if you say yes?" he repeated.

"Mark … are you … yes. Yes," she replied, her hands shaking.

Mark stood and took her in his arms.

She returned the embrace, her strong arms wrapping tight around him. After a few seconds, she stepped back. "My answer is yes, but you know this can't happen for a while, right?"

"I know," he replied. "Not 'til after the bar. I just needed to lock down the hottest law student at this school before some fancy lawyer steals you away."

"Very funny," smirked Sarah. "Now about this vacation?

"We leave in a week so—"

"A week," interrupted Sarah. "I can't go in a week."

"Why not? You turn in your paper on immigration tomorrow then you're off for six weeks?"

Sarah's gaze shifted toward the floor. "I got a call from my unit this afternoon."

Mark's jaw tightened with frustration. "Let me guess, that lazy ass-hat Johnson got out of another assignment, so they called you … and you said yes."

"I did," replied Sarah defiantly. "If I do these two weeks then that frees me up for the rest of the year. It's the best time for me … or it was."

"I don't know why you still do this reserve stuff. Wasn't having a Humvee blown up underneath you enough?"

Sarah took a deep breath. "We've talked about this before, Mark. I can't just … I feel guilty enough for leaving active duty. I just need to stay in touch with—"

"I know," interjected Mark. "And I didn't mean … I know it's important to you. I just wanted to spend the whole summer with my fiancée."

"It's only two weeks," said Sarah, stepping into Mark's embrace again. "I'll meet you then, if you can survive two weeks in the heart of Dixie without me."

Chapter Two

Mark stood at the baggage claim carousel, taking in the scene around him. He was a student of the South; most of his graduate study had focused on it. But it didn't take long for him to realize the South was a place to be experienced, not read about.

To his left was a well-dressed man in his fifties with a thin, blonde woman in her mid-twenties draped on him.

Two Sailors stood behind the couple.

"I'm telling you, dude, there's a fucking alligator living right on the base," said one of the Sailors to the other, his Long Island accent piercing the low roar of the other conversations.

The sound of another New Yorker caused him to turn but as he did, a large man wearing a T-shirt and a trucker hat brushed past him. "Scuze me buddy," he said, the twang in his voice thick to the point of being almost unintelligible.

Now more intrigued by the man in the trucker hat, he turned back toward the baggage claim to see him grab a duct-taped garbage bag from the turnstile. On the back of the man's shirt was a large Confederate flag with the words "Heritage Ain't

Hate" printed above it.

He couldn't turn away. Staring at the shirt, his mind raced as he started to form the foundation for a paper on the resilience of Confederate mythology in his head.

"Mr. Patterson."

Mark turned to see a tall, muscled black man. The man was immaculately dressed in a dark grey three-piece suit. He had amber eyes, a well-kept goatee, and a bald head. The image of one of his father's junior partners instantly came to mind.

"Are you Mr. Patterson?" the man asked.

"Yes," replied Mark.

"I'm Carson Jefferson. I work for the McCleary family. Your bags have been loaded into the car and we are ready to proceed to the plantation at your convenience, sir."

Mark had wondered why his baggage was taking so long. "Thank you … Carson is it?"

"Yes, Mr. Patterson. Carson Jefferson."

"You said McCleary? Do you mean Mrs. Mackey?"

"Of course, sir. But the descendants of Rebecca McCleary still prefer to use the old family name in private circles and always when referring to the old home."

"Very well, Mr. Jefferson."

"Carson, sir," replied the man.

Mark was somewhat uneased by the formality of Carson's behavior. His years as a graduate student had caused him to forget the formality of many elite families. His mind drifted to the stuffy dinners he had to attend as a teenager when his father was entertaining. "No problem, Carson. I'm ready whenever you are."

"Very good, sir. The car is waiting outside. Please follow me."

The heat hit him like a wave crashing on a beach when he stepped into the South Carolina air. He began to sweat almost instantly. "A little warm today," he said, pulling his shirt away from his chest.

"Sir?" asked Carson. "Oh. Yes … it may take you a few days to acclimate to our weather."

"Mr. Patterson," came another voice as he and Carson stopped by a large, black SUV.

"Hello," replied Mark to another black man in a suit.

"I'm Thomas. I'll be your driver during your stay."

"For my stay?"

"Yes, sir," explained Carson. "This vehicle, and its driver, will be available to you at your discretion during your visit to the McCleary plantation."

"How long is the drive to the plantation?" asked Mark.

"About twenty minutes to I-17 and then another thirty until we reach McCleary Lane which is about five miles to the main house," replied Thomas.

"We should be on our way," added Carson, opening the back door for Mark.

Mark climbed into the SUV as Carson sat in the front passenger seat.

"What do you think of Charleston so far, Mr. Patterson?" asked Thomas, shifting the car into gear.

"It's all very interesting, especially for a Yankee."

"Well, Mr. Patterson, if the Old South is anything, it's interesting. I'm sure you'll fall in love with it soon enough."

"I'm sure I will," replied Mark.

Mark watched through the window of the SUV

as they passed from the airport into the crowded evening traffic. The long day of travel soon caught up to him and he began to nod.

A few more miles and he was fast asleep.

The bump of the SUV turning onto a dirt road awakened him.

Rubbing his eyes, he saw the SUV being waived through a security gate manned by an armed security guard. As the SUV passed the security station, Mark looked back toward the guard. He was a tall, stocky man wearing black fatigues with a thick but well-kept beard. The man reminded Mark more of a 'contractor' from the war-torn Middle East than the immaculately dressed doormen guarding most elite neighborhoods in New York.

Turning away from the guard, Mark's attention was drawn to a slow-moving river on the left. He half expected to see an old paddleboat steaming down the channel.

Between the water and the road ran long rows of apple trees.

Looking through the trees, Mark saw an old black man in ragged wool clothing picking an apple from one of the trees. He leaned toward the window focusing on the man …

Mark's heart skipped when the man turned toward him: The man appeared to have no face.

Shaking his head, Mark looked at the man again.

The old man smiled and waved, his face worn and wrinkled, but otherwise normal.

"How long until we arrive?" asked Mark, trying to clear his groggy head.

"Well, technically …" replied Thomas. "… we're there. We've been on McCleary property for the last ten minutes."

"So, all of this …"

Carson turned toward Mark. "The McCleary family has large property holdings throughout the Charleston area with approximately five thousand acres surrounding the original homestead, another fifteen thousand throughout South Carolina, and about fifty thousand total in eight states."

"Fifty thousand acres?"

"The McCleary family has preferred to keep a large portion of their holdings in land and other tangible things, although they do have modest corporate and technology holdings."

"I knew Rebecca McCleary was able to fend off several attempts by speculators to take the plantation after the war but—"

"Mrs. Rebecca was quite a lady," replied Carson. "The family is strong today because of her."

"I'm sure marrying a wealthy Northern railroader after the war helped. With Winthrop Boles in her corner, no one was going to make a play for her land."

Carson's gaze shot back toward Mark. The fierceness in his eyes caused Mark to lean away. "Mrs. Becca didn't need any help, especially from a …" Carson paused, turning away from Mark again. "The McCleary family has always thrived in adversity, Mr. Patterson. And will continue to do so."

"I didn't mean…I meant no disrespect to the McCleary family. It's that same determination and drive that sparked my interest in researching the family. You can see it here," continued Mark, pulling an old book from his backpack. Flipping through the volume, he pulled out the photo of Becca and handed it to Carson.

Carson took the photograph from Mark and

examined it intently. "She was a special lady," he said softly. He looked back toward Mark. "The McCleary family has been very good to mine. After the war, Rebecca McCleary let my family stay on and made sure they had a place to stay so they didn't have to go into the Yankee camps. I'm named after one of my ancestors that worked for her."

"So, your family has been with the McCleary descendants since the Civil War?"

"Since before the war," replied Carson.

"So, you're basically—"

"We are family," interjected Carson. "And we are almost home," he added as the SUV turned down a long road lined with massive oak trees.

"How long is the lane?" asked Mark, peering down a road that seemed to disappear into the horizon.

"About half a mile."

"Shit," mouthed Mark under his breath. He leaned forward to look down the lane. As he did, the form of a colossal antebellum plantation house came into view in the distance.

He'd seen paintings and a few old pictures of antebellum southern mansions, and he'd seen his share of mansions in the North, but seeing the long road lined by massive oaks leading to one of the most iconic symbols of the Old South almost took his breath.

"Magnificent," he said aloud.

"Welcome to McCleary House, Mr. Patterson," said Carson.

McCleary Plantation, February 15, 1865

BAM! BAM! BAM!

The slamming of a fist against the door caused Rebecca to jump with each pounding blow.

"Clara," ordered Henry McCleary. "Run and fetch Carson and your ma. And tell Carson to get my shotgun and load it up."

"Yessa, Massa Henry," replied Clara. She paused, turning toward Becca.

"Now girl!" ordered Henry. "And tell Carson to stay in back 'til I call for him."

BAM! BAM! BAM!

Becca jumped, letting out a gasp. "Papa?"

"I know you Rebs are in there?" boomed a gravelly Irish voice that could only belong to a Yankee. "Open the door or we'll knock it down."

"Papa? What are we gonna do?" pleaded Becca.

"Don't fret, Becca," replied Henry. "They probably just want to know if any of our boys came this way."

Becca had heard the horror stories about what Yankees would do Southerners. They were savages. "But I heard they—"

"Hush girl," ordered Henry.

BAM! BAM! BAM!

The door rattled as thunder boomed again. "Last chance, Rebs," roared the voice on the other side. "Open the door."

***

Stepping out of the air-conditioned SUV, the heat and humidity weighed on Mark like a heavy coat. Taking a deep breath and stretching his arms, he looked around. To his left was a massive two-story barn painted brilliant red with white trimming. Behind the barn was a long horse pasture and beyond that a large field of cotton. The view to his right was as equally iconic. Several acres in size, the field was heavy with mixed rows of corn, potatoes, squash, and other staple crops. "It's like a painting," he said to himself.

"We do try to keep the place presentable," came a soft, smooth voice with a light drawl.

He turned to see a thin, blonde woman walking down the long stairway from the main entrance to the house. Although he assumed she was in her late forties, she was fit and tan. She could easily have passed for thirty-five.

"It really is beautiful," replied Mark.

The woman smiled and extended her hand. "I'm Brianna Mackey. And you must be Mr. Patterson."

"Yes. Please call me Mark. I hope it isn't too forward, but I had expected … well … you look much younger than I had envisioned."

"Aren't you sweet," replied Brianna.

"I'm sorry if that was inappropriate, Mrs. Mackey," said Mark. He knew Southern concepts of social norms were sometimes peculiar, and he was a novice.

Brianna laughed. "You're fine, honey," she said, leaning in close. "Your first piece of advice about the South: Never apologize for giving a lady a compliment."

"Of course, ma'am," replied Mark with a smile.

"Well, okay then," said Brianna, feigning surprise. "I've gone from looking young to ma'am in less than a minute."

Mark knew his face had to be turning red. "I … uh …"

"I'm just pullin' your tail, sweetie. Call me Bri,"

interrupted Brianna, placing her hand on his back. "Carson and Thomas will handle your bags. Why don't you follow me inside?" asked Brianna as her hand gently moved down Mark's back.

"Yes, ma—Bri," replied Mark.

As Mark followed Brianna through the house, there was too much for him to take in. Every room looked like a museum, filled with antique furniture, décor, and artwork. Looking into what could only be called a receiving parlor, he saw an antebellum painting over the fireplace. It was a young man wearing the uniform of a Confederate cavalry captain. The painting was amazingly detailed, the man's blue eyes almost glowing and the gold trim off the officer's braid seemingly jumping off the canvas.

"Your home is incredible, Mrs. Mack—"

Brianna turned around quickly.

"Bri," said Mark, correcting himself.

Brianna responded with a smile before motioning toward a woman in a maid uniform who was standing at the entrance to the parlor. The woman was beautiful with caramel skin, amber eyes, and thick curly hair. "You can thank Clara for the condition of the house." Brianna placed her hand on Clara's arm. "She's been with us for years."

Clara stepped forward and picked up a serving tray from a small round table. "Welcome to the McCleary House, Mr. Patterson. Would you like some cookies and tea?"

"I'd love some tea," replied Mark. "And maybe a little sweetener?"

Clara tilted her head in confusion. "Sweetener, Mr. Patterson?"

Brianna snickered. "Oh, honey. This is South Carolina … *everything* down here is already sweet," she said with a wink.

"Of course," said Mark as he took a glass of tea. Placing the glass to his lips, he took a deep refreshing drink. The sweetness of the drink caused him to close one eye and clinch his teeth. "That's really sweet."

A loud 'thud' echoed down the hallway, startling Clara and sending the pitcher of tea crashing onto the floor.

The pitcher shattered, sending shards of glass flying.

Mark turned to see one of his suitcases had tipped over, causing the noise. Turning toward Clara, he saw her on her hands and knees, frantically sopping up the tea with a rag.

"Sorry, Mrs. Mackey," she pleaded.

"Don't fret, Clara," replied Brianna. "Accidents will happen." Brianna turned toward Mark. "Clara can be a little jumpy at times … especially with new people in the house."

"Sorry, Mr. Patterson," added Clara, looking up from the floor. "Sometimes the house—"

"Your leg," declared Mark, seeing a small piece of glass embedded in her calf.

He reached out to examine the wound.

"No!" snapped Clara, grabbing Mark's arm.

Looking into her eyes, a chill shot down his spin. "I …I was just—"

"I'm fine, Mr. Patterson," said Clara, directing his arm away from her. "I'm sorry for spilling the tea."

"That's okay, Clara," interrupted Brianna, placing her hand on her shoulder. "You leave that for now and go have that looked at," she added.

Brianna looked back toward Mark as Clara left

to attend to her wound. "This house has a lot of history. Sometimes if you think about it too much …" She paused, glancing toward the painting over the fireplace. "We can talk more about that later. Let's get you settled in."

***

McCleary House: February 15, 1865

BAM! BAM—

The front door of the McCleary House blasted open, letting wind and rain pour into the foyer.

Becca's heart stopped as a large Union solider with sergeant's stripes stepped into her home. Lightning again illuminated the house, causing Clara to let out a scream.

Henry stepped in front of Clara and Becca, holding his old musket. "Get out of my house," he ordered.

"I told ya boys. Rebs are like roaches. They like hiding in the dark," said the sergeant with a smile.

"This is our property, Yankee filth," spat Becca, her voice low in a combination of defiance and fear.

The sergeant's gaze landed on Becca. "Looky here, boys." He slowly examined her from head to toe.

Becca *felt* his eyes consuming her.

"Another Reb bitch that thinks she's too good for us," he continued.

Becca stepped backward, further behind her father. She'd seen Yankees before; prisoners at the train station in Charleston and working with the slaves on road gangs. They'd all seemed so weak and helpless, but the sergeant and two soldiers with him were large, towering over her frail father. Looking into the sergeant's eyes, she felt like she was looking into soul of the devil himself.

"Get off my property," said Henry again. "Just let us be."

"It ain't your damned property anymore, Johnny Reb," replied the solider to the right of the sergeant. "This farm..." The man glanced toward Becca, sending a shiver down her spine. "... and everything on it belongs to the Union Army as contraband of war."

"Everything ..." added the second soldier, spitting tobacco onto the floor. "... including prissy little Reb bitches."

Becca's father repositioned himself between her and the second soldier. "You stay away from—"

A gunshot rang through the room.

"Papa!" screamed Becca as her father's head snapped backwards.

Becca fell to her knees beside her father, his limp body collapsing to the floor. Throwing her head toward the ceiling, she let out a guttural scream.

"Lookout!" yelled one of the soldiers as Carson burst into the room with a gun.

Another shot rang out and the sergeant fell to one knee as the room erupted in a torrent of gunfire.

Becca curled into a ball on the floor, screaming.

As quickly as the chaos had started, it was over.

"That fucking darky shot me," grumbled the sergeant, pushing himself back to his feet.

"Don't worry, Sergeant. We got him," reported one of the soldiers as he reloaded his Sharp's rifle. "Guess his day of jubilee has come."

Becca opened her eyes to see her father on the floor next to her, blood pooling underneath his head. Tears began to flow down her cheeks. "Papa!" she moaned.

"You okay, Sergeant?" asked the second soldier.

"Just a few pellets, that's all. You two go check out back."

The men moved past Becca and her father, but the sergeant remained.

"These fucking Rebs gotta learn they ain't masters of shit anymore," he grumbled, looking down at his injured leg then toward Becca.

She looked up at him defiantly. "You deserve worse … murderer!"

The sergeant's face tightened and his mouth curled into a snarl, reminding her of a wolf before it attacked. He stepped toward her and she began to scoot backwards.

"Com' ere," he grunted, grabbing her hair.

Becca cried out in pain as he yanked her to her feet.

"Where's the silver and gold, bitch?"

"You rot in hell, trash," she growled, spitting in the sergeant's face.

The sergeant pulled her close. "Fucking plantation whore," he spoke through rotten, tobacco-stained teeth. "You're gonna regret that. I'm—"

His attention was drawn toward the returning soldiers. They were dragging Clara, kicking and screaming, into the room,.

"Look what we found out back, Sergeant."

"She tried to run when we shot the other one," added the second solider.

Seeing her brother lying dead on the floor, Clara let out an ear-piercing screech. Her screams were silenced by a blow from the butt of a rifle. Clara fell to the floor and let out a low moan as she struggled to stay conscious.

"Shut up," laughed the soldier that knocked her

to the ground. As he looked down on her, he stopped laughing. He curled his mouth as his hand moved down to his groin. "Sergeant, can we take her for ride?"

The sergeant, still holding Becca by her hair, looked over Becca's shoulder toward Clara, who was slowly rising to her knees. Whimpering, Clara tried to crawl away, but the second soldier shoved her back onto the floor.

"You boys have your fun," said the sergeant. "Then dump it in the swamp along with the one that shot me."

"Me first," declared the man that had killed Carson, dropping his rifle and undoing his pants."

"No!" shouted Clara but the other soldier crashed his boot into her jaw.

"No, you just hold still, honey-child," said the second soldier as he knelt down and grabbed her arms.

"Please …" begged Becca. "Just take what you want!"

As Clara's screams fill the house, the sergeant pulled Becca's face close to his. "Oh, we will, missy." A flash of lightning illuminated his face, accentuating his dark eyes. "Now it's your turn, my little Carolina peach."

"You'll have to kill me first," she spat.

She became nauseated as the sergeant's powerful hand slid down her back.

"I ain't gonna kill you, little bitch." He paused as he looked over her body. "But you're gonna wish I had." He pressed Becca's body against his, running his rough tongue over her cheek. "Tonight, I'm gonna see what a fancy, rich little peach tastes like."

Disgusted, she spit in his face again.

Her vision blurred as a blow from the sergeant's fist sent her tumbling to the ground. She let out a loud grunt when he drove his boot into her stomach, sending her flying.

Hitting the ground, she began to sob from the pain.

"Let's go, little peach," said the sergeant.

Becca cried out as he grabbed her hair and dragged her across the floor.

She struggled, grabbing at his arm to relieve the pain in her scalp. "Let me go!"

The sergeant remained silent as he pulled Becca over the rough hardwood floor. At the parlor room he stopped, and in one motion pivoted and tossed her into the room. Laying on the floor, she looked up at him.

"Missy, you're gonna be my slave tonight," he said, pulling the doors closed.

The piercing sound of Clara's screams shifted to muffled sounds.

"Please. No!" pleaded Becca, grasping at the crucifix around her neck as thunder rolled through the house.

***

"Hopefully these accommodations will suffice," said Brianna as she and Mark entered the bedroom.

"It will more than suffice," replied Mark.

"This was Becca McCleary's room. You have a view of the horse pasture through this widow and over here …" Brianna threw open the curtains and opened a window on the left side of the room. "…from here you can see where Saligi Swamp runs into the back of the property." She turned back toward Mark. "Don't let the word swamp fool you, though. It's very beautiful during the day. And some say very romantic at night."

Ignoring Brianna's remark about the swamp being romantic, Mark changed the subject. "How old is this desk?"

"It was Virginia McCleary's. Best we can tell it's as old as the house."

On the desk sat two old leather-bound books. Mark opened the cover of the first book. It read: *PLANTATION AND FINANCIAL RECORDS, HENRY MCCLEARY 1831-1840.*

"The family records?"

"Yes … well, part of them. Once you are finished with that one I can bring you the next. There are four other volumes covering the period you mentioned in your letter."

"Thank you. And this one?" asked Mark as he opened the cover to see the words: *DIARY OF BECCA MCCLEARY.* "Her diary," said Mark quietly, running his fingers over her name.

"Why, yes, Mr. Patterson. That's why you're here, right?"

"Yes. Of course," replied Mark, looking up from the diary.

"Well then, I'll leave you to it, Mr. Patterson. Clara has prepared some items for you in the kitchen for you to have at your leisure. Formal meals will start tomorrow at 7:00, 12:00, and 6:00, if you choose to join us. Carson and Clara live on the property and have a small cottage just beyond the pasture. They usually retire around seven o'clock, but if you need them, there are call buttons throughout the house. Also, if they're unavailable, there's an on-call staff member and handyman available in the main service building a few miles away."

"So I have the whole place to myself?"

"Normally you would. We usually only stay at the Old Home a few weeks every season. Our main home is of course in Charleston. But my daughter, Rebecca, informed us she would be coming in from her semester in London earlier than expected. My mother and grandmother also decided it would be a good time for all of the family to get together so we will be here for the remainder of the summer."

"Rebecca," said Mark. "Rebecca. Just like—"

Brianna let out a quick laugh. "Yes. We McCleary girls like to honor our ancestors."

"Of course."

"But don't worry about us; we'll try not to be too much of a bother."

"I'm sure it'll be no bother but thank you."

Feeling tired from his travels, he began to wonder what the time was. He pulled his cell phone from his pocket.

There was no signal available.

"Oh, I forgot to tell you we have limited access to the internet and cell service in the main house. If you need access to anything of that nature I have contacted the head of the History Department at the University of Charleston. You will have full access at their facilities if you need them."

"Thank you, Mrs. Mack-Bri. But if I might ask, I would think a family as involved in the modern world as yours would have better connectivity."

"Oh, we've tried. We've run lines on several occasions and they always go down. We're able to get connectivity at the main services building most of the time and we can make direct land-line calls from the kitchen." Brianna placed her hands on the bedroom wall as the harsh sound of cawing from crows outside could be heard. "Just seems like this old house pushes back against new things. Even the power is from local generators and solar panels placed throughout the property."

"It definitely has that 'Old South' feel to it."

"Yes, *she* does … Just the way we like it."

"Would it be possible for me to use the connection at the services building tomorrow to contact my fiancée?"

Brianna's head snapped toward Mark. "I wasn't aware you were engaged."

"Just a few days ago. If it would be okay, I was planning on having her join me here in a few weeks."

"Here? At the house?"

Mark realized he may have asked for too much. Southern hospitality was a real thing, but it also was a tricky thing. "Of course, if that is a problem, I can—"

"Don't be silly," replied Brianna, regaining her composure. "No one will say we're not hospitable to visitors. Even if they are Yankees."

"I, uh—"

"Oh, silly. I was just playing with you a bit. We Southerners may love our history, but most of us do know it is just that, history. Your fiancée, what is her name?"

"Sarah Barkley. She's doing her two weeks of military duty right now but—"

"She's a soldier?" asked Brianna, her mouth tightening.

"A captain in the reserves. She was on active duty for six years but she's in law school now."

"Your fiancée is a soldier and a lawyer from New York?"

"Yes. She's very accomplished."

"You Northerners have very different ideas of

what makes an 'accomplished' woman."

Mark could tell the comment was meant to be a slight, but a subtle one. "She's in the top five percent of her class and is a decorated combat veteran," he replied in defense of Sarah.

"I meant no offense, Mr. Patterson. It's just been a long time since a Northern soldier has been in the McCleary house. And they were most definitely unwelcome …" She paused. "But of course, Sarah is more than welcome here."

"I don't want to take advantage of your hospitality. If it's a problem—"

"Of course not. It was just a surprise," said Brianna, a smile painted on her face. "Now, if you'll excuse me, I need to get ready for Rebecca's arrival."

"Of course. And thank you again."

Brianna stepped to the other side of the bed and opened the other window. "You'll want to keep both windows open. It creates a nice cross-breeze that helps with the heat."

Looking around the room, she placed her hands on her thin waist. "That should about do it. I'll see you for breakfast in the morning. Goodnight, Mr. Patterson."

"Goodnight, Bri," offered Mark and Brianna left the room, shutting the door behind her.

Mark let out a heavy sigh. It had been one hell of a first day.

The breeze moving through the room was comforting and he moved closer to the window.

He stuck his head out of the window.

The chirp of crickets and the groaning of frogs sounded louder than downtown Syracuse traffic. At the edge of the swamp ran a lighted row of lamps lining a walkway to a small dock.

As he looked on, Clara came into view. She stopped halfway to the dock and turned quickly, looking up toward Mark. Her expression was empty and vacant as she stood motionless for seconds that seemed like moments.

The sudden sound of a horse neighing from the opposite window drew Mark's attention.

He turned toward the sound of the horse but a splash in the water from the other window caused him to look outside again.

Clara was gone.

Leaning out of the window he looked round. "Weird," he said with a shrug. "Guess I should get to work," he added to himself, turning toward the desk and the McCleary family books.

He pulled out the old chair and sat.

The chair squeaked and cracked as he shifted his weight and pulled the chair forward toward the desk. "Here we go," he said, resting his hands on the Rebecca McCleary's diary. He had waited a long time for this. Taking a deep breath, he opened the diary.

He read the first passage:

Secret and private thoughts of Becca Anne McCleary

April 8, 1856

Papa says I can't play with Clara any more. He says it is not proper for a lady. Why was it proper when I was 11 but not 12? I don't care what Papa says, I know Mama will let me.

A smile came to his face as he flipped to the middle of the diary:

June 15, 1859

I miss Robert. I don't know why he must be at school with all those Yankees at West Point. Papa says it's good for him and it will help him run the plantation after his time in the

Mark closed the book, "Hmm," he murmured as he contemplated all the great stories that must be between those two passages. He opened the diary again, starting at the beginning.

After a few moments of sitting in the old, creaky chair Mark rose and moved to the bed to continue reading.

Not realizing how tired he was from trip, he was soon asleep with the diary lying on his chest.

***

In his dreams, Mark envisioned Sarah on top of him, straddling his body.

"I've been waiting for this for a while," said Sarah as she pulled her shirt over her head. She leaned forward, kissing him before sitting up again and undoing her pony tail. He hair fell over her shoulders, framing her beautiful face. "You just lay right there," continued Sarah as she unbuttoned Mark's shirt.

Mark closed his eyes and let out a low moan as she began to kiss her way down his chest and stomach until she reached his shorts.

He looked down toward her.

His gaze met her's when she looked up toward him. "And it's not even your birthday," she said with a smile, pulling down his shorts and lowering her head.

"God," moaned Mark.

He was soon lost in a fog of pleasure as she took him in her mouth.

"Will you die for me?"

"What?" asked Mark.

"Will you die for me?" came a voice that wasn't Sarah's.

Mark looked down, his hands buried in the hair of a girl that wasn't Sarah. Startled, he pulled her head up to see her face as he slid away from her.

The girl was a beautiful blonde girl in her early twenties with a crucifix necklace around her neck.

"Who are you?" demanded Mark, scooting his body against the headboard.

"We were meant to be together," replied the girl, crawling toward him.

"Yes," came another woman's voice.

Mark spun to his left to see Clara standing next to him, holding a knife.

"Together forever," said Clara as she stabbed downward toward Mark.

***

Jumping from his sleep, Mark frantically scanned the room.

It was empty.

"Holy shit," he said aloud as he took in deep breaths to calm himself.

Slowly settling his nerves, he rose and walked across the room to a pitcher of lemon water. Taking a glass from the table, he filled it. As he drank, he noticed the drawer of the desk was partially open.

He opened the drawer.

"No fucking way," he said, again quickly scanning the room before retrieving a crucifix necklace.

Chapter Three

After a night of restless sleep, Mark made his way from his room to the breakfast table. Coming down the stairs, the smell of bacon invigorated him and he picked up his pace. At the entrance, he paused. Several women's voices could be heard. Mark stood outside and listened.

"Nana, you just don't understand how things are today," said a woman with soft, but defiant, South Carolina accent.

"You don't sass your nana, Rebecca," replied a voice he knew to be Brianna.

Beginning to feel awkward, Mark turned the corner and entered the dining area.

Four women were sitting at a large breakfast table. Clara was pouring a cup of juice for the oldest lady, who appeared to be at least in her eighties.

"Good morning, ladies," said Mark.

The conversation stopped as they all turned toward him.

The woman sitting with her back to him turned last.

Mark's heart skipped a beat … she was the spitting image of the girl from his dream.

"Good morning, Mr. Patterson," said Brianna.

"Good morning," replied Mark, his gaze still locked on the young woman.

"Let me introduce everyone," continued Brianna. "This is my mother, Bessy Lawson, and this is Nana Baily Farmington, my grandmother. And this sassy young lady is my daughter, Rebecca."

Rebecca stood and gave Mark a quick kiss to each of his cheeks. "Welcome to the McCleary House, Mr. Patterson. Or can I call you Mark?"

"Rebecca Mackey!" said Bessy, scolding her granddaughter.

"Oh, Grammi," replied Rebecca, taking her seat again. "It's nothin'. That's how people in France say hello all the time."

"Your mama warned you about givin' sass, girl," replied Bessy. "Just 'cause you've been to France don't mean you need to go kissin' every boy you see. If everyone was jumpin' off bridges, would you?"

"If there was a cute boy at the bottom I might," replied Rebecca, glancing toward Mark with a flirtatious smile.

"Now you stop playing with our guest and behave Rebecca Mackey; he's engaged to be married."

"Engaged?" Rebecca cast a confused glance toward her mother before turning back to Mark. "I didn't mean anything by it."

"It's okay," replied Mark still off-balance from the woman in his dream sitting in front of him. "I …"

Rebecca rose from her chair again, her gaze focused on his hand. "What is that?"

"It was in the desk in my room," replied Mark, presenting the necklace.

Before he could react, Rebecca snatched the necklace from his hand. Holding the chain, she let the crucifix rest in her palm. "This is mine." She turned toward Brianna. "Mother, it's *the* necklace.

"It can't be," replied Brianna, standing to inspect the piece of jewelry.

"It is," said Rebecca, holding the necklace up to her face. "I know it." She turned back toward Mark. "Where was it again?"

Mark felt sweat begin to roll down his forehead and his body grew warm.

This didn't make sense. "I …" He paused as he flashed back to Rebecca looking up toward him in his dreams. "It was in the drawer of the desk in my—in Becca's room."

"I've been looking for this for a long time. I thought it was lost forever."

Rebecca's eyes were wide and welling up as she continued.

"This was given to Becca McCleary by her mother Virginia on her deathbed. A McCleary woman has worn it ever since."

"Until our world traveler misplaced it," added Bessy.

Rebecca looked into Mark's eyes as a smile replaced her somber expression. "But it's back now," she said, embracing him. "Thank you so much for finding it."

As he felt her body against hers, he couldn't help but think of the dream again. She couldn't hold him much longer or his body would begin to react.

"You're welcome," he said, shifting his waist away from her body.

Rebecca slowly released her embrace and stepped back slightly, her hands still holding Mark's.

He smiled back, unsure of what to do next.

"Well enough about that necklace," said Brianna.

"Rebecca, sit down and behave."

Brianna then turned to Mark. "Mr. Patterson, please have a seat."

The only chair left empty was the one next to Rebecca.

With a smile, Mark took his seat and looked up to see Clara standing next to him.

He jumped slightly, the less-pleasant vision from his dream flashing through his mind.

"Are you okay, Mr. Patterson?" asked Clara.

"Yes, thank you," replied Mark, quickly regaining his composure. "How is your leg?"

"Sir?" asked Clara.

"The glass from yesterday? Is it …" He paused as he looked down toward the location where the glass had been stuck in Clara's calf. The was no sign of an injury. "You don't even have a scratch."

"Oh," replied Clara, shifting her leg so he could no longer see the area where the wound had been. "It really was nothing."

"But it—"

"Would you like some coffee or juice, Mr. Patterson?" asked Clara before he could complete his sentence.

Apparently, she didn't want to talk about it. "Juice, please."

As Clara poured the juice, Bessy spoke.

"So, Mr. Patterson, your father is Justice Patterson?"

Mark quickly swallowed the first bite of food he'd placed in his mouth. "Yes, ma'am. He is."

"I met him several years ago."

"Really?" replied Mark. "I had no idea."

"His firm did some legal work for the family in the early 90s."

"I wasn't aware. Hopefully you were satisfied with my father's work."

"It was just a little property issue up North, if I remember. But your father did an excellent job."

"He usually does."

"I'm surprised you didn't follow him into law, Mr. Patterson," added Brianna.

And there it was. The question Mark had heard his entire life. He took a quick breath to repeat what was by now a rote answer. "A lot of people expected me to, but I just wanted to do something different ... on my own."

"I've heard he has been ill," said Bessy.

Mark wondered for a moment how they knew about his father's recent bout with cancer. But then he remembered Brianna Mackey was the matriarch of one of the wealthiest and most influential families in the country. "Uh, yes. But he is doing better the last few months."

"That's good. I'll have a card sent to him."

"That's very nice of you."

"Brianna says you are here to study our family history?" asked Bessy.

"Yes, ma'am. Well, your history and that of a Union unit that disappeared around your plantation toward the end of the war."

Brianna placed her cup on the table as the sound of hounds barking outside echoed through the room. "So, your research extends beyond our little family?"

"Actually, my interest in your family history came about after I started researching the missing squad."

"Missing squad?" asked Rebecca.

"Oh, yes," replied Mark, excited to talk about his research. "A squad of cavalry from the 125th New

York was on a reconnaissance patrol near your plantation on February 15th, 1865. They left in a storm just at dusk and were never seen again."

"How dramatic. No wonder you're researching it … seems like a great mystery story," said Brianna.

"That was the night Charleston fell," added Rebecca.

"Yes. Yes, it was," said Mark, surprised by the beautiful young woman's knowledge of the date. "Very impressive, Rebecca."

"Any respectable Southern lady knows her history. And besides, it is one of my majors."

"You're a history major?"

"Yes. I start my senior year at Duke this fall."

Excited by the opportunity to talk history, Mark continued. "What's your area of concentration? Are you planning on going to grad school?"

"I'm double majoring in U.S History and Economics … little of the old South and the New. I plan on applying to UNC to study Southern History for my masters."

"Really? I could put in a good word—"

Brianna and Rebecca chuckled in unison.

"Sorry, honey," said Brianna. "We didn't mean to be rude. It's just that a member of the McCleary family doesn't need a recommendation from well, excuse me for saying, a Yankee to get into a southern college."

"But thank you, Mark," added Rebecca with a smile.

"Rebecca, watch your manners," warned Brianna.

"It's okay if I call you Mark, isn't it?" asked Rebecca.

"Of course."

"Well, thank you for joining us, Mark," said Brianna. "But if you'll excuse us, we old ladies are going into Charleston for a charity auction," she added, rising from her chair.

"Yes. Of course," he said as Brianna stood.

"And what are your plans, Mr. Patterson?" asked Brianna.

"I think I'll keep going through the diary and the records you left and maybe have Thomas take me to the services building so I can check my email."

"Oh, I'm sorry," huffed Brianna. "Thomas had to run out for some errands this morning. But I'm sure Rebecca can give you a ride."

"You're not going to Charleston?" asked Mark.

"To a stuffy auction? I'll pass. I was just gonna hang out at the old house today. I guess I can find time to give you a ride."

"That would be great. Thanks."

***

Mark stood in front of the McCleary House, waiting on Rebecca. He noticed his foot was nervously tapping on the deck. His heart quickened as he tried to make sense of his awkward, but exciting introduction to the young woman. "Calm down," he told himself, glancing at the screensaver of Sarah on his phone.

The roaring of an engine and screeching of tires drew Mark's attention from his phone.

He looked up as Rebecca's car slid to a stop in the driveway.

Rebecca McCleary definitely made it hard for any man to 'calm down.' Driving a silver BMW convertible, she wore a pink bikini top and short, cutoff jean shorts.

Mark couldn't help but take a second to observe

the beauty of her toned, tanned body as she pulled herself up with the frame of the windshield.

"Hey!" shouted Rebecca over the blaring pop music. "Get in!"

Mark, shaking his head to get the thought of her body out of his mind, walked to the passenger side and sat next to her.

"You ready, Mark from New York?" she said over the music.

"Yes. Thank—"

The squealing of tires drowned out the music as Rebecca floored the car, causing it to drift slightly before she steadied it out on the main road.

"Let's get you there quick like a bunny," she said, with a smile. "After three months in dreary old London, I need to get as much of this South Carolina sun as I can."

Mark smiled in reply and turned back toward the road, trying to focus on anything other than the beautiful woman next to him as the car raced down the road.

But that wasn't going to be possible.

"So how long will ya be at the service building?" asked Rebecca. "I can wait for you if ya want."

"I have to check on a few emails and see if I can call or skype Sarah."

Rebecca brushed her hair away from her face. "Sarah? Is that your fiancée?"

"Yes," replied Mark, holding up his cell phone to show Rebecca his screen saver.

"Pretty," declared Rebecca dismissively. "What does she do?"

"She's in law school."

"A lawyer? Bet your daddy's happy."

"He doesn't know we're engaged."

"He doesn't know?" asked Rebecca, turning her attention away from the road long enough to concern Mark. "Really?" She laughed, finally tuning back toward the road just as Mark was about to warn her she was drifting off the road. "Now that would never happen down here … not in proper families."

"I just haven't told him yet. We were just engaged a few weeks ago and he just started feeling better—"

"I heard Nana say he was sick. What was wrong with him?"

"He just finished his last round of chemo a month ago."

Rebecca looked toward Mark again. "Cancer?"

"He's doing better. Hopefully they got it all."

"Well I hope so too," said Rebecca, placing her hand on his leg.

A jolt of electricity ran up his leg. "Thanks," replied, focusing on the road on front of them.

A few long seconds passed before Sarah removed her hand. "So, when are you getting married?" continued Rebecca.

"It will be a while. I have another year before I defend my dissertation and Sarah has one more year of school before she starts preparing for the bar … that's if she doesn't volunteer to deploy again."

"Deploy?"

"She's in the Army reserves."

Mark's comment brought another long glance from Rebecca.

"So, wait … your fiancée is a Yankee, a lawyer, and a soldier?"

"Yes."

She laughed, shaking her head. "Don't let Nana Bailey hear that. She's Old South. No doubt she'd start talking about Virginia and Rebecca McCleary rolling over in their respective graves."

"Is it really that big of a deal?"

"Not to me. But c'mon Mark, you're a historian. You have to know we Southerners don't like to let go of our history ... especially lost causes." She gave him a coy smile. "Just like we Southern ladies like the idea of going after something we shouldn't."

Mark looked at her profile as Rebecca returned her focus to the road. It was like he was looking at a real-life version of Becca McCleary.

He turned away. He had to stop thinking about it ... about her.

After a few long seconds, he saw the service building come into view.

"Oh, here we are," said Rebecca.

Mark grabbed the dash, his body bouncing against his door as Rebecca whipped the convertible into the parking lot and came to a stop.

"See," she said with a smile as she gently patted Mark's knee. "Quick like a bunny."

"Thanks," replied Mark, hopping out of her car.

"No problem, Mark," said Rebecca.

She reclined her car chair and slid her sunglasses over her face. "I'll be here waiting for you when you're done with, what's her name again?"

"Sarah," replied Mark.

"Okay," said Rebecca as she pulled her glasses down her nose and gave him a wink. "I'll be out here ... when you're ready for me."

Mark smiled.

"Whew," he mouthed as he turned away and made his way into the service building.

***

The service building was very clean, everything

in its place. Tools and equipment were stacked neatly and a big dry-erase board on the back wall listed a series of tasks assigned to the service staff.

"Can I help you, Mr. Patterson?" asked a middle-aged man in work coveralls as he sat at a small desk near the entrance.

"You know who I am?"

"Mrs. Brianna runs a tight ship, Mr. Patterson," said man, holding up a clipboard with the first few pages flipped back to show a photograph of Mark. "And she likes the help to know who her guests are."

"I see," replied Mark. "How long have you worked here … uh … Tom?" asked Mark, reading the name on the man's coveralls.

"About thirty years now I guess."

"How often have they had guests?"

"Oh, not very often … you should consider yourself lucky."

"I do."

Tom placed his hand on Mark's shoulder. "And what brings you to the service building? I'm guessing the internet."

"You would be right."

Tom pointed to a hallway to Mark's left. "Just take a left and stop at the first door on the right. There's a small office in there where the family and their guests can get access."

"Do I need a password?"

"Becca," replied Tom.

"What?"

"That's the password: Becca."

"Well that's simple enough," said Mark. "And a bit on the nose."

"Hey, I just work here, Mr. Patterson," said Tom with a smile.

"Thanks," said Mark before turning and making his way to the small office.

Inside the room was a moderately-sized wooden table with a computer and printer set on top.

Mark sat down and turned on the screen. "B…E…C…C…A," he said out loud as he typed in the password. Pulling up his email, he skipped over some messages from the university and opened an email from Sarah.

Hey Babe,

Hopefully your research is going well. Things here are … well, the Army. We have a new major and he's a pain in the ass. We're headed out in a day for an exercise, so I'll be out of touch for about a week. I'd rather just run through the range and do some power points this time, but Major 'Tightass' is all 'Train like you fight.' Which is funny because he's never seen a day of combat.

Anyway, I gotta head out for a run but sent a few pictures of your sexy soldier.

And stay away from those Southern girls :)

Mark opened the attachment containing several pictures. He smiled as the first picture opened. It was a selfie of Sarah in her uniform. Next, he opened pictures of her with her unit. Scanning the pictures, he noticed a man in uniform with his arm around Sarah in one picture.

He opened the next one.

In the picture Sarah and the man were singing into a beer bottle together.

The last photo was a group photo with the man standing behind Sarah with his hands on her shoulders.

Mark clicked the reply tab and started to type.

Who's the guy?

He stopped, shaking his head. "Don't be that

guy, Mark," he said to himself.

He deleted '*Who's the guy?*' and started typing again:

Hey soldier-girl -

Things are fine here ... the plantation is really something to see ... hopefully you'll love it. The South is a different world, that's for sure.

Stay safe.

Can't wait to see the future Mrs. Patterson again!

Mark moved the cursor over the *send* button and let out a sigh. Sarah was often the target of the men she worked with … and why wouldn't she be?

He clicked the mouse to send the email.

She was smart, brave, and beautiful. It had been the source of more than one argument between them, but Mark knew he could trust her and that she could definitely take care of herself. But that was only half the problem. She was a decorated combat veteran and he was a doctoral student, an academic. Despite his faith in her, he still worried about all of those alpha males constantly surrounding her.

He let out another heavy breath and closed his eyes. The vision of Rebecca in her bikini top and jean shorts popped into his head.

Mark laughed; he shouldn't be worried about Sarah with the vision of Rebecca's tan body running through his mind.

He turned off the monitor and left the room.

Passing Tom, he gave a wave.

"Enjoy your stay, Mr. Patterson."

Mark smiled and turned toward the door just as two other workers entered. The men were younger than Tom, in their early twenties. Both were looking back at Rebecca, who was still reclined in the car in the parking lot.

"God-damn, that's not even right," said the first man.

"Don't even waste your time thinking about it. We could put all of our money together and would still be about seven zeros away from having a shot at that," replied the second.

"Don't mean I ain't gonna think about it—"

"Sorry, guy," said the man as he realized Mark was waiting at the door.

"No problem," replied Mark, sliding between the two and making his way outside.

Pop music still blasting from the radio, Rebecca slowly raised her seat into position. Sliding her sunglasses down again, she smiled. "Ready for me now?"

"Uh … yeah," he stammered. "Finished with the computer."

"That was quick. Didn't get to chat with your girl?"

"No. Just emails."

Rebecca slid her sunglasses back into position. "Well hop in, Mr. Mark, I've got a long day of tanning to get back to."

Mark opened the car door and sat. As soon as he pulled the door shut, he was thrown forward and then back in the seat as the car jumped backward and then sped out of the parking lot.

As she pulled onto the main road, Rebecca began to sing along with the music.

He couldn't help but watch as Rebecca bounced up and down in her seat to the rhythm of the song as she sped down the road. She was like a tornado. A really hot tornado.

"So what ya doing the rest of the day?" she asked.

"I will probably try to get through more of Rebecca McCleary's diary. I—"

"Lookout!" he yelled, seeing a goat in the middle of the road.

Rebecca hit the brakes and swerved.

Mark felt like his stomach was floating as the car went sideways and slide to a stop in the gravel along the side of the road.

Mark looked back toward the goat, still standing in the road. It was black with a heavy ragged coat. He noticed one of its horns had grown downward as well. Looking at the beast, he realized it was also staring at him.

An uneasy felling came over him.

"Are you okay?"

Mark's gaze, and attention, was still locked on the goat as he looked into its yellow eyes.

"Mark?"

Finally, Rebecca's voice got his attention and he turned toward her.

"Uh, yes. I think so," he replied. Rebecca's cheeks were flush, and her breathing was accelerated from the excitement. "Are you okay?"

"I'm fine," she replied, glancing toward the goat. "Damn things roaming around all over the place … hope a gator gets it."

Mark saw the fire and intensity in her eyes as she spoke. When she turned toward him, he was still looking into her eyes.

Shifting his gaze, he saw something over her shoulder, just off the road. Examining the area more, he realized it was a partially overgrown road. "Where does that go?"

"That's the road to the family cemetery," answered Rebecca, her voice still elevated after their run-in with the goat.

"The family has a cemetery on the property?"

"Sure," said Rebecca, her voice now calm. "Where else is a McCleary gonna be buried?"

She took a deep breath then spun her body toward him. "Wanna see it?" she asked.

"I should get back to the diary …" He passed. He wondered how many people had the chance to see the McCleary family plot? "Sure. Why not?"

"Alright then," said Rebecca, turning the wheel sharply and pulling onto the old road. "Just watch out for goats."

Rebecca continued, talking over the crunch of the car's tires on the gravel drive. "When I was in high school I used to ride my horse out here." She looked at Mark. "Do you like to ride, Mark?"

"Never ridden before," he replied. "My dad used to take us to Saratoga for the races, but we never owned any."

"You're missing out," she replied with a smile. "Maybe I'll teach you to ride this summer."

"That would be nice."

Mark noticed the sound of the gravel road had given away to the soft swishing of tall grass.

He also noticed the absence of the normal sounds of the forest. No birds chirping. No squirrels chattering. Nothing.

"Oh, we're here," said Rebecca as she let the car roll to a stop in front of a white fence at the entrance to an immaculately kept cemetery in a small clearing in the forest.

Mark got out of the car and walked to the gate. On the arch of the gate was a sign that read: ABSOLUTLEY NO ADMITTANCE WITHOUT FAMILY PERMISSION. He looked down to see a lock on the gate. "It's lock—" He turned to Rebecca just as she was pulling a T-shirt over her bikini top.

"Of course, it is," she replied as she shook her key chain. "I've got a key."

"Why is it locked? It's in the middle of your land."

"You would keep a safe locked in your house, right?"

"I guess I—"

"Well, what's in there is more precious than anything in any safe our family owns."

"I understand," said Mark, remembering the power of family bonds in families like the McCleary's. "But why is it all the way out here?"

"It seems like a long distance the way we came," said Rebecca as she unlocked the gate. "It actually isn't that far from the main house. The road curves around ..." She pointed to opposite side of the cemetery. "... there's a trail on the other side that leads to the swamp that runs to the back of the main house."

She swung the gate open and stepped inside.

Mark paused. "You're sure it's okay to—"

"Sure, Mark. It's okay as long as you're with me."

At his feet was a clear cobblestone path winding between the headstones. The path expanded, encircling the cemetery.

He stopped at the first headstone. It read *Becky Boles 1868-1960*.

"She was Nana Bailey's great-great grandmother. Turned nineteen on the day of big earthquake in 1886."

"That's right, there was a big earthquake in Charleston."

"And there's Nana Bailey's mother, Bethany. Born in 1912. The same year the *Titanic* sank, with her daddy on it."

"Really?"

"He was a banker from Manhattan and had some shares with White Star, so he wanted to make the maiden voyage."

Mark saw a headstone with Brianna's name and birth year etched on it. "Your mother has a headstone already?"

"We all do. See … there's mine," said Rebecca, pointing to a headstone with her name and birth year on it.

"Isn't that a little macabre?"

"Not at all. This is our land … we're part of it." She gave him a look as if she was talking to a child. "It's not like we would be buried anywhere else." She paused, looking around the cemetery. "I actually think it's nice to know where you're going to be for eternity … which is here with all the McCleary women.

"What about the men?"

"Mama says it's because their families wanted them buried back up North. And since McCleary women are buried here—"

"So, a cemetery just for women?"

"Except for two," replied Rebecca as she motioned for Mark to follow her.

She walked to the opposite end of the cemetery to three headstones set apart from the others. Stopping at the headstones, Rebecca bowed her head slightly.

Mark saw the names. The first was Robert McCleary. The dates *1841-1863* with the word *Gettysburg* below them were etched into the stone.

"Becca McCleary's brother, Robert. He was killed in Pickett's charge."

Beside Robert's grave was a large headstone with

two names on it: Virginia and Henry McCleary. Under Virginia's name were the dates *1815-1860* and the words *Beloved Mother.* Under Henry's headstone read: *1812-1865 Murdered by Yankee Invaders.*

A chill ran down Mark's spine. There was no doubt few people, especially Northerners, had set foot on this hallowed shrine to Southern pride and loss.

"Henry and Virginia McCleary," said Mark as he squatted next to the headstone. "Murdered by Yankee invaders."

"You have to know he was killed by—"

"I didn't. It's not in the records anywhere."

Mark noticed Rebecca subconsciously rubbing the crucifix on her necklace between her fingers.

"And his daughter, Becca, had her grave dug right over there where she could look over the whole place."

"You're really in tune with your history," said Mark.

"Well of course I am," huffed Rebecca. "If you don't know where you come from, you'll never find out where you're supposed to be going."

Mark was fascinated with the story. And Rebecca Mackey. "I have to ask …"

"What is it?"

"The jokes and the playing around? You're obviously a smart girl. Why do you—"

Rebecca laughed. "Have fun? Because I can. Just because I'm smart and rich …" Rebecca tilted her head slightly. "… maybe not humble. But either way I know that soon I'll be going to board meetings and dealing with the family business. And I'll gladly do it. But that's not a good reason to be some tight-ass prissy caricature of a Southern belle you'd read in some cheap romance novel."

"I guess I—"

"Don't you want to have some fun before you become a stuffy old history professor? I can see you now, tweed jacket and bow-tie …"

Mark laughed. "C'mon now."

"You brought it up."

"I guess you're right."

"Of course, I am … I'm brilliant," said Rebecca holding her hands out to her sides. "Now let's get you back to your research, Professor Mark. And while you're at it, maybe you can learn to not judge a book by its cover," she added with a smile.

Chapter Four

Later that night, Mark sat at the desk in his room, flipping through pages of Becca McCleary's diary. He stopped on an entry dated July 5, 1863:

Papa said there was a big battle up North in Pennsylvania. He said he doesn't know who won but it was big. I know he's worried about Robert but he won't say anything to me. I know God will keep him safe.

Having read the tombstone early, Mark's stomach tightened. It was over a century and half later, but a sense of loss washed over him.

He started to turn the page but stopped. He'd read diaries before … ones that had conveyed great loss by the author. But now he felt as if he were intruding on Becca McCleary's privacy. "C'mon, Mark," he said aloud after exhaling heavily. "You're a historian … this is what you do."

Reassuring himself of his purpose, he turned the page:

July 8, 1863
Robert's dead. Those damn Yankees killed him.

There were no more entries until July 20, 1863.

Papa won't leave the parlor except to go to Robert's room. Clara brings him food and Carson has made sure the other slaves keep to work for now but he can't stay like this. We got word that Robert's body would be shipped but Papa was too drunk to go into Charleston so I wrote Carson a pass and sent him into town to make the arrangements for his arrival. I guess it's just me and Papa now.

I wish I could just drink too. All I can do is go to my room and cry. Robert was brave and strong and fighting for our freedom from those Yankee devils ... and they killed him. Every night I pray for God to strike down that monster in Washington and those blue-bellied butchers. If I was a man I'd enlist so I could take my revenge. No death is too horrible those Yankee murders.

As Mark read the entry, his skin grew hot and his pulse quickened.

He was angry.

"Whoa," he mouthed, shaking his head. Why was he angry? The pain felt by Becca was real but both her and her brother and father were on the losing side in a fight to free millions of people from slavery. Realizing he'd lost objectivity, he closed the diary. "That's enough for tonight," he said aloud as he rose from the desk and prepared for bed.

It wasn't long until Mark fell into a deep sleep.

He began to dream.

Sitting in a posh restaurant similar to ones his father dragged him to whenever he was home, Mark took a drink of his scotch. As the alcohol warmed his body, he looked around the restaurant.

At another table sat Sarah and the man from her

email photos. The man leaned in close to Sarah, his mouth next to her ear. They both laughed.

Mark took another drink.

Sarah looked up and waved before turning her attention back to the man at the table.

"Mark." He heard Rebecca's voice and turned to see her sitting next to him.

"Are you ready to order, honey?" she said with a smile.

"Can I help you, Mr. Patterson?"

Mark turned to see Clara in a waitress uniform.

Clara smiled and drove a knife toward him.

Mark jumped out of his dream.

"Goddamn it," he cursed, rubbing his face to wake himself. He picked up his phone to look at the picture of Sarah.

It was dead.

"Damn it, Sarah. Why couldn't you just come with me?" He lay back in the bed, staring at the ceiling.

***

Rebecca ran her hand over the mane of Nox, the powerful jet-black Arabian in the McCleary stable. The horse shuddered nervously and neighed at her touch, its eye flashing toward Rebecca.

"Malacia!" grunted Rebecca in Latin as she gripped the mane tightly.

The horse settled, and she tightened the straps of the saddle.

"And where are you going?"

Rebecca turned to see Brianna standing at the entrance to the stable. The dim light of the stable shone on Brianna's angry face.

"I'm going for a ride. I need to clear my head," she replied, turning her attention back to the saddle.

"What you need to do is stay on task, Daughter."

Rebecca snapped her head toward her mother. "You think I don't know that?" she replied in a low voice, glowering. "And no one said anything about a fian—"

"That is irrelevant, my dear," replied Brianna with a cold smile. "You have to—"

"I know what I have to do, Mother," interrupted Rebecca.

"Then you best get to it."

Rebecca pulled herself onto Nox. She felt the nervous power of the horse underneath her.

Then she felt Brianna's hand on her leg.

"This is always the most trying time for us McCleary women," she said with a reassuring smile.

"Don't worry about me." Rebecca directed Nox away from her mother. "I know what's at stake," she added.

"I should hope you do. That's why I am curious about why you are out joyriding when there are things that need to be done."

Rebecca looked down at her mother with a tight, malevolent smile. "I said I know what I am doing. And we both do enjoy our joyrides, Mother," she hissed. "At least mine has good breeding."

Brianna returned Rebecca's smile. "Well, Daughter. At least mine doesn't need the lash to please."

Rebecca gave the reigns a hard jerk causing the horse to turn toward Brianna again. "That's your problem, Mother … the lash is half the fun," she added before giving Nox a kick, causing him to leap forward and trot out of the stable into the darkness.

***

After a restless night, Mark made his way down the stairway toward the kitchen. Even though he could hear the women talking in the dining area, he didn't stop.

He had other plans. And he wasn't ready to see Rebecca—or Clara—yet. Instead, he walked past the flurry of voices and outside where the driver, Thomas, was waiting for him with an SUV.

"Where to, Mr. Patterson?"

"University of Charleston History Department, please."

"Yes, sir," replied Thomas as he opened the door for Mark.

***

Mark sat in a deep leather chair in the reception area of the History Department, his arms awkwardly high compared to his torso. He pushed against the arms of the chair, trying to pull himself up; as he did, the sound from the rubbing and bending of the leather sounded unnecessarily loud.

Clearing his throat, he looked around the room.

Splitting the seating area was a glass bookshelf stacked with publications from the faculty. On the opposite wall was a row of pictures showing the heads of the department all the way back to when it was called Morris Harvey College at the turn of the last century. Glancing at the table by his chair, Mark saw the department's monthly newsletter. A picture of Brianna standing beside the current head of the history department was on the front page. The title of the article read: *ENDOWED CHAIR FOR SOUTHERN HERITAGE FULLY FUNDED.*

The sound of a heavy wooden door slamming startled him.

Mark turned to see a tall, thin man in his mid-twenties.

"You must be Mark," said the man. "I'm Lee

Hampton, a second-year grad student. I was, uh, volunteered to show you around."

"I didn't want there to be any fuss," replied Mark as he stood to shake Lee's hand. "I just wanted to check out some of your archives."

"It's no big deal. Actually, it gets me out of looking up census data for Professor Rickman," said Lee, forming a pistol with his hand and placing it to his temple. "Follow me. I'll take you to the library."

"So, your dad's Justice Patterson?" asked Lee as the two made their way out of history building into the quad.

"He is," said Mark.

"And he's okay with you becoming a history professor?" He glanced toward Mark as the two continued to walk. "You do know there's no money in this field, right?"

"He still thinks it's just a really long pre-law path," said Mark, not sure why he was opening up to Lee. "You know, the ten-year path to law school."

"As long as he pays the bills, right?" said Lee.

"I've paid for my education through grants and scholarships," replied Mark. "He hasn't paid for a thing since my undergrad."

"Sorry, man," replied Lee. "I didn't mean to … I guess I just assumed with all that money—"

"I'm doing this on my own."

"Gotcha," said Lee. "And I didn't mean to offend you, but you gotta know how many broke-ass grad students would love to be in your position."

"Is that the library?" asked Mark. He hated this conversation … mostly because he had to have it with every grad student he'd ever spoken to when they found out his father was so wealthy … and powerful.

"Yep. Here we are," said Lee as they stopped at

the entrance. "You must have some powerful local friends too," said Lee, opening the door for Mark. "The Department Chair himself came down to the grad student break room and asked me to show you around. And that stodgy old bastard never leaves his office."

"I guess Brianna Mackey got in touch with him."

Lee's head snapped toward Mark. "The McCleary family?" Lee let out a laugh. "That'll do it. How do you know them?"

"I'm researching a Union patrol that went missing near their plantation the night Charleston fell."

"Oh. I thought you might be researching the deaths."

"Deaths? What deaths?"

Lee chuckled. "You know, like every man that has married a McCleary woman has come to an … uh … untimely end. Every one of them since the Civil War."

"Seriously?" How did he not catch that?

"Look it up yourself. Every single one."

"Do people think they've killed their husbands?"

"I don't think so. It's all been natural causes or accidents. But the more superstitious locals think it's some kind of Gullah curse. You know, for owning slaves back in the day."

"Gullah curse? The old lowland slave culture?"

"Yeah. They call it Hoodoo. Kind of like black magic or witchcraft.

"Seriously? Witchcraft?"

"Hey, I didn't say I thought it was witchcraft. But you must remember, for some people down here, the supernatural is just part of their lives."

"Hey, Mary," said Lee to a middle-aged woman

sitting behind a counter. "Dr. Summers reserved the Civil War collections room for Mr. Patterson."

"He sure did," replied Mary. "It's already opened. Do you need me to show him where it is?"

"I can show him," said Lee. "Thanks."

"Just let me or one of the staff know if you need anything, Mr. Patterson."

Mark smiled. "I will. Thank you."

Mark followed Lee up two flights of a spiraling staircase and down a long hallway to the southern wing of the library.

"Here you go," said Lee, pointing to a set of glass double-doors. A plaque above the door read ANTEBELLUM & CIVIL WAR COLLECTIONS. To the right of the door was another plaque that read AVAILABLE THROUGH A DONATION FROM THE MCCLEARY FOUNDATION FOR SOUTHERN HERITAGE. Through the doors Mark saw several large wooden cabinets to the left, a set of microfilm and microfiche projections, three computers on the opposite wall, and a large reading table in the center of the room. In the center of the table was a bronze statue of a Confederate flag bearer leaning forward, as if charging an unseen Union position. The entire right side of the room was one large wooden bookshelf filled with what appeared to be period books.

"Over there ..." said Lee, pointing to the bookshelf. "... are the *Official Records*. Maps of Charleston and South Carolina are over there, as well. Some private collections including diaries, letters, and business records are in this section, too."

"Thanks."

Lee placed his hand on Mark's shoulder. "But if I was you, I'd start off by looking up all their husbands' death certificates. And watch out for that McCleary Hoodoo," he added with a smile.

***

Mark wiped his tired eyes as he sat at the computer. Several books and maps were scattered on the table behind him, but he was too distracted to focus on his initial line of research. He was too far down the rabbit hole.

He hit *enter* and the search engine for archived newspapers soon listed several articles. He looked at the first to post. It read *HARRISON MACKEY, CHASE MANHATTAN EXECUTIVE DIES IN PRIVATE PLANE CRASH.*

Mark wrote the name and date on a notepad to his right. He then examined his notes, reading them aloud.

"Winthrop Boles … Boles Iron & Steel … 1868 … fever. Malcom Moore … B&O Railroad, 1893 … drowning. Justin Slayton … banker … White Star Lines … Titanic." He paused. "Damn," he mouthed then continued. "Hawthorn Farmington … shipping … torpedoed in the North Atlantic … 1942. Dwight Brandt … Lawyer … 1956 … car accident. Representative Robert Lawson ... 1979." He shook his head. "Anaphylactic shock from … bees?" He placed the pad back on the desk. "Holy shit." Lee was right. Every single husband of a McCleary woman since the Civil War had died shortly after marrying.

He put his pen to the pad and wrote *Gullah Curse?* at the top of the pad.

***

'Gullah Curse.'

The thought kept running through Mark's consciousness as he sat at the dinner table listening to the McCleary women talk about world events and the

61

local gossip.

Visions of each of their husband's deaths played out in his mind.

"Mr. Patterson," said Brianna, taking him away from his thoughts.

"Yes, Brianna?"

"Are you with us, honey?"

"Oh, yes. Sorry. I'm just—"

"How was your research?" asked Bessy.

"Very informative, Mrs. Lawson. By the way, Dr. Summers sends his regards to the family."

"I bet he does," laughed Brianna. "Old coot doesn't want to lose any of that McCleary Foundation grant money."

"What did you research today?" asked Rebecca.

Mark turned toward her. Her golden hair was pulled up in a tight ponytail and she was wearing a tight tank-top shirt that showed just enough cleavage to avoid being distasteful.

Around her neck was the crucifix necklace.

"I'm looking into several aspects of local history and …" He paused, unsure if he should ask. "Well, if it's too personal let me know. But—"

"What is it?" asked Brianna

"I just … it seems like there is a bit of a rumor about your plantation being cursed."

The room fell silent as each of the women turned their gaze on him.

"Those stupid rednecks are talking again, aren't they?" spat Bessy Lawson.

Mark instantly regretted asking the question. "I'm sorry, I shouldn't have—"

"Oh, don't worry about it. We could care less what the trailer-trash in North Charleston thinks." Brianna placed her fork on her plate. "Look around,

Mr. Patterson. Does it look like we are cursed?"

"Not at all. It was just that I noticed most of the marriages—"

"Our husbands die young," interrupted Brianna, her face tight. "Is that what you were going to say?"

"I—"

"It's okay—"

"This isn't proper dinner talk, Brianna," said Bessy in what Mark interpreted as a warning.

"It's okay, Mama. He's new here, and his job is to ask questions. So, I'm going to give him answers."

Brianna turned back toward Mark. He could tell she was irritated but painted the smile of a Southern belle on her face as she continued. "Our family, as you know, is both wealthy and influential. That makes some people jealous. These people then come up with crazy stories and the lower class just sops it up like gravy. I'm assuming you've been looking into the deaths of the men in our family?"

"Yes, but—"

"Then you know there was never a speck of evidence that anything other than God's will had anything to do with their deaths. Our husbands' deaths are something to mourn, not fodder for all those carpetbaggers in Charleston to talk about."

"The same goes for those fools talking about magic and—"

"Now Rebecca, we'll have none of that blasphemous talk in here," interrupted Bessy.

"I was just saying it was stupid, uneducated gossip. I didn't—"

Brianna's gaze tightened on Rebecca, stopping her mid-sentence with a word leaving her mouth.

Rebecca sat back in her chair.

"I'm truly sorry for bringing it up, Mrs. Mackey,"

said Mark. "I shouldn't have been so forward as to speak of family matters as an outsider."

"It's okay, Mr. Patterson. I just want to make sure you don't get wrapped up in all that Charleston nonsense. The McCleary family has an excellent reputation and it's frustrating when people try to damage what we have struggled to maintain for generations. You have no idea what reputation means to one down here."

"I understand. And let me say your family has been more than gracious to me."

Mark waited for a reply, but an awkward silence hung over the table.

"Okay," said Rebecca, breaking the silence. "That was an, uh, interesting conversation. May I be excused, Mama? I want to head out to the wild flowers before dark."

"Of course, honey," answered Brianna before turning toward Mark. "And you, Mr. Patterson, what are your plans for the evening?"

Between his emotional response to Becca McCleary's diary last night and his ill-fated plunge into the deaths of the McCleary women's husbands, Mark figured he could use a break from research. "I thought I'd go for a walk before and maybe clear my head."

"Oh, that's an excellent idea. You should take the trail down by the horse pasture. It runs along the lower half of the property."

"And watch out for witches and ghouls," added Rebecca as she rose from the table. "At least according to—"

"Rebecca!" said Brianna. "That is enough."

Rebecca cast a quick, defiant glance at her mother. "Hmmm. I'll be out by the wild flowers."

***

Unable to shake the stories of the deaths of each woman's husband, Mark's mind wandered as he walked down the wooded path. Even if it was just a series of unfortunate consequences, it was still hard to believe.

But each death made sense. A car accident. An owner in the White Star being on the Titanic. A shipping officer killed in WWII. Alone they all fit…except maybe the bee attack.

But murder? It was too much of a stretch.

Mark let out a chuckle. "Then it must be witchcraft." He'd only been in the South a few days and was already a superstitious fool. He needed to get back on task and focus on his actual research, not some wild supernatural goose-chase. Or on Rebecca Mackey.

A flicker of light drew his attention to the trees above him. The sun was starting to sink into the tree line.

"Time to get back," he said aloud. He knew he was too much of a city-slicker to get stuck in the South Carolina woods at night. Turning to retrace his steps, he started back toward the house.

It wasn't long until darkness began to envelop the path in front of him. He looked up to see flashes of orange and yellow as the sun disappeared behind the trees. "Damn it," he grumbled as he began to quick-step. Soon the path was devoid of sunlight and Mark picked up his pace again. With each step it seemed the path grew darker.

Focusing on the quickly disappearing flashes of red light through the trees, he didn't notice a snake in the trail until he was about to step on it. "Shit!" he cursed as he stumbled backwards, falling to the ground.

Even he knew what the unmistakable rattling meant. "Damn it. Damn it Damn it," he mouthed as he scooted further away and slowly stood. "A fucking rattlesnake? Really?" he panted.

He looked back down the trail. It was so dark.

The roll of thunder shook his body and the wind began to pick up. Looking into the trees, he saw the leaves begin to turn.

A storm was coming.

"Come on," he said, looking away from the ominous trail and back toward the path to the house. "Seriously?"

The snake was still there.

His pulse quickened and he began to look frantically for something—anything—to help him get out of his situation. His eyes fell upon what looked like an older, overgrown path to his right.

The snake rattled again.

"Damn it."

He turned back toward the main path. A few feet down the trail, it was already pitch black.

Thunder rolled again, and a heavy drop of water hit his arm.

"Fuck it," he cursed, turning to head down the overgrown path.

The wind blowing through the leaves sounded liked hushed voices calling to him and every branch or brush that rubbed up against him sent a jolt of fear down his spine out of fear that it might be another snake or some insect. "Shit. Shit. Shit," he said to himself with each step.

A loud screech took his breath and caused him to jump. Falling into thick brush, he saw a large owl burst from a nearby tree.

"Goddamn it," he panted as he scrambled to get

out of the bushes.

Taking a deep breath, he looked up to see a break in the path up ahead. In the disappearing light, he could see a field of wildflowers a few hundred feet ahead him. Focusing on the only remaining area of light, he ran to the edge of the field.

Taking in much needed air, he saw a jeep with the hood popped up on the opposite side of the field.

Then he saw her.

Rebecca, wearing the white tank-top and cut-off jeans, was leaning over the jeep's engine. He couldn't help but look at her muscular legs and tight stomach as her shirt rode up her torso.

"Oh, c'mon," he huffed, shaking his head.

He just couldn't get away from her.

Mark turned back toward the trail. It was a pitch-black. He looked back toward Rebecca as she backed up from the jeep and kicked the fender.

Behind her, black clouds rolling in as the last flashes of red and yellow flickered on the horizon as thunder again rolled over the field.

"Just see if you can help and get back to the house," he said to himself. "That's all you're gonna do Mark Patterson."

As he spoke, Rebecca saw him and waved for him to join her.

"Into the valley of death ..." he said as he began to walk toward her.

"You must be lost, professor!" she called out as he approached.

"I think I am. But I'm guessing you're not."

"No," she grumbled. "But this piece of ..." She kicked the jeep again. "Do you know anything about cars?"

"Historian," replied Mark, raising his hands in

the air.

"Alright then; we're hoofin' it," declared Rebecca, slamming the hood shut and adding one more kick to the broken-down jeep.

A drop of water hit Mark's arm. Then another.

A clap of thunder shook Mark to his bones as the rain began to pour.

"Quick. Follow me!" shouted Rebecca, grabbing Mark's arm. "Over here."

Rebecca pulled Mark through the field as he struggled to watch his footing and not Rebecca's back-side.

"Here," she said, drawing his attention to an old, run-down shed.

The rain intensified and began to sting Mark's face and hands as he rushed to keep up with her.

When they reached the building, she opened the door. "Get in," she ordered.

Mark hopped over the threshold and into the old shed just in time for another boom of thunder.

The sound of the rain on the metal roof was a dull roar as he tried to focus his eyes in the darkness of the shack.

Rebecca's body pressed against his, startling—and exciting—him. "Sorry," she said as she placed her hand on his chest. "This shed should have power … I think there's a light in here somewhere …"

Her breath on his neck sent a tingling sensation through his body.

"Here it is."

Mark closed his eyes when the room filled with light, but they flashed open as a large cat hissed and leapt past him, disappearing into the rain.

"Son of a bitch!" huffed Mark. "I'm really getting sick of animals coming from … from everywhere today," he continued, regaining his composure.

Rebecca laughed. "Can't fix trucks. Afraid of animals. You really are a city boy," she said with a smile.

As Mark looked at her, her blond hair was dripping wet as it fell over her shoulders. He then realized Rebecca's white shirt was soaked through, making it nearly transparent.   Mark wished she hadn't found the light so that he wouldn't have the temptation to look.

"Uh ... You found me out," he said, turning his gaze away from her and looking around the interior of the shed. Tools, bags of seed, cans, and other normal farming and gardening equipment was spread throughout. In one corner was a row of candles and grass baskets on a small table. Wanting an excuse to not look at her, he walked over to the baskets.

Inside the basket were the aged, scattered bones of a small animal, probably a rodent. Above the table odd symbols were painted on the wall.

As Mark inspected the odd scene, Rebecca rummaged through a stand of shelves. "These storms pass over quickly. It should just be a few minutes until—"

"What is this?" he asked, still fixated on the collection of bones.

"Oh," replied Rebecca with a laugh. "That's really old. I didn't even know that was still here. It's been so long."

"But what is it?"

"Oh, it's just some silly magic thing Clara and I tried back when ... I must have been a sophomore in high school."

"A spell?" asked Mark, the words 'Gullah Curse' flashing into his thoughts.

Rebecca tittered. "Yeah. Clara and I heard all the rumors about the family, so I looked up a Hoodoo spell on the internet and we tried to get back at a girl in class. Mama found out …" Rebecca shoot her head. "… she wasn't happy."

"Did it work?"

"Did what work?"

"The spell?"

Rebecca glared at Mark with a smirk painted on her face. "Really? That's stuff's just a bunch of wives' tales and cheap magic tricks. All it did was stink up the place and almost burn this shed down … not to mention get me grounded for a month and a talk with Pastor Jenkins."

"So, no dark arts for you? No revenge spells or love potions?"

Rebecca laughed. "Ah, no. You know about my family; we don't need spells to get revenge." She stepped in close. "And I don't have any problems in the love department, Mark."

"I guess you wouldn't," he said as he looked into her eyes.

She looked back, smiling.

He wanted her. He knew it was wrong and he wouldn't do anything about it. But he did want her.

He let his eyes shift down to her soaked shirt and then back up hers.

She met his gaze and smiled.

The pounding of the rain on the roof suddenly stopped.

"We should probably get back," he said half-heartedly.

"Should we?" asked Rebecca, placing her hand on his arm.

"We should."

But he didn't move. Looking into her eyes, the word 'DON'T' just kept repeating in his mind.

Finally, he forced himself to take a step away from her. "It's getting late."

Rebecca frowned but quickly regained her composure, replacing it with a smile. "Well then, don't just stand there, follow me," she said, tugging on Mark's arm.

Mark followed Rebecca outside and they made their way back to the jeep.

Leaning into the glove box, Rebecca pulled out a flashlight. "C'mon," she said, smacking the side of the flashlight.

Nothing.

She gave the light another smack and it illuminated.

With the light working, she began to search the back of the jeep. "Hopefully it didn't get soaked. There it is," she said, pulling a flannel shirt from underneath the seat. "You ready to go?" she asked as she slid her arm through the shirt.

"Lead the way."

"Well, keep up. I'm pretty sure you would die if you were left out here overnight," she laughed.

***

Mark, still soaked from the rain, laughed as he and Rebecca walked up the stairs of the McCleary House.

"Well, at least you didn't die out there in the middle of the swamps. You're practically a pioneer now."

"I'm sure I could've made it for a few more hours."

"Unless there's another stray cat out there waiting to do you in."

Mark laughed to hide his embarrassment as they reached the second floor. "Well I guess I should thank you for saving my life then."

"No big deal. You can just call me your own personal superhero," said Rebecca as she raised her arm in a muscle-man pose. "To the rescue ... all you need to do is call."

"Sounds good to me."

Rebecca's expression transitioned from playful to a more serious tone. "Does it, Mark?"

He looked into her eyes again. What was it that ...? "I think I'm gonna call it a night."

"Okay?" replied Rebecca softly, her eyes returning his gaze.

"Okay, then. Goodnight, Rebecca."

"Goodnight, Mark," she said with a smile as she started to turn. "Oh," she continued, spinning back toward him. "I almost forgot. Get with Carson tomorrow so you can be fitted for your costume for this weekend."

"Costume?"

"Oh. They probably forgot to tell you. Since we're all at the House this summer, my mother has decided to put on a ball to raise money for the Heritage Foundation."

"A ball?"

"Yeah," replied Rebecca, her eyes dancing. "We're all gonna dress in costume and have an old fashion Southern ball."

"Really?" Mark had heard of that sort of thing but didn't think they were real.

"Oh yeah. They're so much fun." She leaned in close. "And mama makes a killing for the Foundation at $5000 a plate."

"Damn." Mark doubted his grant would cover

that.

"But you're a guest so it's free for you."

"So, everyone just kind of parades around like it's 1850?"

"Pretty much. Well more like 1862 … I think that's the year mama picked."

"Then I'm in," he replied.

"Awesome," said Rebecca.

He felt a jolt of electricity shoot down his spine as she leaned forward and kissed him on the cheek.

"Would you mind playing my escort?"

"I don't know if it would be appropriate," he stammered. "I'm—"

"Oh, it'll be okay," said Rebecca. "I just don't want any of the local boys getting any ideas and if you would just play along …" She looked up him, a coy smile on her face. "If it won't be too horrible for you?"

"I would be honored," he replied.

"Great," she snapped, giving him a quick peck on the cheek again. "It's a date!"

"Wait … I …"

She had already turned and was on her way back to her room.

Damn it," he said under his breath, watching her walk away. "You're gonna get yourself in trouble," he murmured to himself.

Shaking his head to get the thought of Rebecca in her wet shirt out of his mind, Mark slowly opened the door to his room. As he stepped inside, he saw Clara, on her hands and knees, backing out from under his bed.

"Clara?"

"Oh. Mr. Patterson," replied Clara as she rose. "I was just finishing up your room. Mrs. Mackey wants it cleaned at least twice a week."

"No problem, Clara. Thank you."

The *chirping* of crickets outside punctuated the silence as Mark let his thoughts drift to his recent nightmares and Clara's role in them.

"I'll be leaving now, Mr. Patterson. Unless you need something?"

"Oh, no. Sorry, Clara. Thank you."

Clara gave a slight bow of her head to Mark. "Have a good night."

***

Mark's dreams did little to help him forget about Rebecca. Every time he drifted off, his dreams were of him and her together. After awaking the first few times, he no longer felt bad about the dreams. He just wanted to get back to sleep … to dream again.

The loud cawing of a crow startled Mark, awaking him again. Looking to his window, he saw the bird look at him before flying away.

"Damn it, Mark," he said to himself. "Get your shit together."

He laid his head back on the bed. "Sarah," he said. "Sarah."

***

The rhythmic beat of house music reverberated against Lee Hampton's body as he walked through the crowded party. Entering the kitchen, he saw his friend, Jesse Colson at the snack table. Jesse was average height and weight—average everything. Lee was sure if Jesse would stand in one place long enough, he'd just disappear into the background of whatever was behind him.

"Lee!" shouted Jesse over the music, waving for him to come over.

"What's up, Jess?" he asked.

"Oh," answered Jesse, shoving a handful of nuts into his mouth as he spoke. "Not much … just checking out the crop."

"Yeah," laughed Lee. "Summer session is pretty dead but there's still more than enough eye candy."

"And most are juniors or seniors so they're over that freshman fifteen."

"I love being a grad student. It makes picking up undergrads so much easier," continued Lee, popping a peanut in his mouth. "You just play the experienced, helpful mentor … it's like honey for juniors and seniors who are tired of obnoxious frat boys."

"Like fish in a barrel," agreed Jesse.

Two girls walked up to the table. One was a petite blonde girl with short hair wearing a short floral summer dress; the other was a brunette with her hair up in a pony-tail wearing a form-fitting black top and tight white pants.

"Hey, ladies," said Lee. "What brings you out tonight?"

The girls stared at him blankly for a second before the brunette spoke.

"Oh … we're just here with our boyfriends," she said.

"Yeah," added the other girl. "Just getting them some snacks."

"Oh," said Jesse. "What—"

"We should probably get back to them," said the brunette.

"But nice meeting you," said the blonde, driving the nail in the coffin.

"Okay. You too," said Lee, his voice trailing off as they walked away.

He watched as the girls stopped a few feet into the living room to talk to three other girls.

"Yep," declared Lee. "Fish in a bar …" Looking past the group of girls his eyes landed on a beautiful woman in a denim skirt and tight white T-shirt leaning against the wall.

Their eyes met and he smiled.

She smiled back and began walking toward him. She had perfect caramel-colored skin, amber eyes, and her hair was shoulder length and full of tight curls.

"What the fuck is happening?" asked Jesse. "Is she coming over to you?"

"I think so," replied Lee, his gaze still set on the gorgeous woman on a few feet away."

"Hello," he said over the thumping of the base. "My name's Lee."

"What?" she said, smiling wide.

"I'm Lee," he repeated, slightly louder. "Are you an undergrad?"

"I don't go here," she replied glancing toward Jesse.

"Well," said Jesse, understanding the cue. "I should be going." He turned toward Lee. "Have fun, buddy," he added, giving Lee a pat on the back.

"Maybe we should go into another room where it's not as loud?" offered the woman.

"Sure," blurted Lee.

The woman took Lee by his hand and led him to a small utility room. Shutting the door, the pounding of the music subsided to a dull, repetitive echo.

"I didn't get your name?" he asked.

"Clara," she replied.

"You said you weren't a student. What are you doing at the party?"

"I'm hunting," she replied with a snap of her teeth and a smile.

Lee smiled back. "And what are you hunting?"

"Whatever comes in my sights that suits me, honey."

"Oh," replied Lee, unsure of how to act with a woman like her. "I teach at the——"

Clara pressed her body against his, wrapping her arms around his torso. "Honey, I don't care what you do," she said. "I'm not taking resumes tonight."

Lee leaned in and kissed her. As he did, she pulled him in closer, rubbing her body against his.

He could swear she tasted like cherries.

She broke their embrace and looked up toward him.

Her amber eyes were fixed on him. "Wanna show me your place?"

***

Lee moaned as Clara, leaning against the apartment door, kissed his neck. "Just let me … get my keys."

It took longer than he expected to dig out his keys as each kiss sent a jolt of excitement through his body. Finally, he unlocked the door and they backed into the room as he kissed her.

Once inside, he stepped back and looked into her eyes; they were devouring him. "I just want you to know nothing is going to happen tonight that you don't want to——"

Clara's finger pressed against his lips, silencing him.

"Don't waste your breath, dear. I'm not one some fragile schoolgirl." She leaned in and kissed his neck again.

Lee grunted in pleasure as she bit down on his neck.

"And don't you worry. I want *everything* that's going to happen tonight," she said, almost growling.

Clara gave Lee a gentle shove and straddled him as he fell back onto the couch.

"You ready for the good stuff, baby?" she asked.

"Oh, I'm ready," he replied.

"Good. Just gotta get something outta my pocket."

"I'm all about being safe," said Lee with a smile. "I—" Lee jerked backwards as Clara presented a hypodermic needle. "I'm not into—" He tried to push himself upright on the couch, but Clara slammed his torso back onto the couch. He tried to struggle but she was too strong. "What? Hey—".

"Shut up," she snarled, jabbing the needle into his neck.

Hot liquid shot into Lee's veins, the heat and pain expanding quickly through his body. "What the fuck did you give me, bitch?" demanded Lee as Clara released her hold, allowing him to stand.

"I'm just teaching you some manners, Charleston trash."

Lee's head became heavy. He stumbled. "You … what …?"

Clara grabbed him, holding him upright even though his legs had given out. "You think you can talk trash about the McCleary family and ruin their reputation?"

She released Lee and he staggered, falling against a bookshelf and collapsing onto the floor.

"Wh …" He couldn't form the words.

The room began to spin and his vision blurred as saliva leaked from his mouth onto the cold linoleum floor.

Lee had no control of his muscles when Clara grabbed him again, this time lifting him to his feet with a single hand. His mind screamed but his body wouldn't respond as she dragged him to the window of his fifth-story apartment. Pushing the window open with her free hand, Clara lifted him into the opening.

"Too bad you can't handle your drugs. Then maybe you wouldn't have fallen out of your window."

Lee's heart pounded, his eyes pleading for her to stop. "Pl … please."

"Goodbye, trash," said Clara coldly as she shoved Lee from the window.

Chapter Five

Mark tugged at the heavy tie pressing against his neck as he waited for Rebecca. Looking at the mirror in his room, he let out a chuckle. He'd tried for half an hour to get his cravat knot right before he had to call for Carson, who did the work in just a minute. And although he felt like he was in a sauna, it wasn't much worse than the normal South Carolina heat, the thin cotton undershirt offering a little comfort under the heavy vest and thick wool tailcoat.

What was definitely *not* comfortable were the tight leggings clinging to his legs. And if the leggings weren't squeezing him enough, his feet throbbed in his tall leather boots. He almost wished he could wear the Confederate officer uniforms he had heard some of the men in attendance would be wearing, but even he knew how blasphemous that would be.

The sound of period music began to echo through the house as the band hired by Brianna began to play. He tugged at his vest as he looked at himself in the mirror again. At least he would look the part of the Southern planter class—until he opened his mouth and his New York accent destroyed the façade.

A knock on the door drew his attention and he shuffled to open the door.

His heart stopped when he saw Rebecca.

She was wearing a full-length baby-blue dress with white lace trimming. The wide hoop-skirt angled up perfectly to her small waist, made even smaller by a corset that was no doubt underneath. The dress was cut low enough so that her breasts were pressed close together. He followed her body past the crucifix necklace to her perfect jaw-line and soft lips, which were formed into an inviting smile. Her hair was flat on top but flowed down into a series of tight curls running down to her shoulders.

He closed his eyes and opened them again to make sure it was really her. "You look just like Becca," he said without thinking.

"Thank you," replied Rebecca. "I'll take that as a compliment."

"It is," said Mark. "And I really mean it. It's like she stepped out of the picture into real life."

"C'mon," said Rebecca, her cheeks growing flushed.

"You're magnificent," he said unable to hold back.

"Okay," laughed Rebecca. "Maybe we should just go downstairs and join the others," she added, holding her arm out to him.

"Oh, yes," he said, realizing he needed to present his arm so they could make a proper entrance downstairs.

As she took his arm, Rebecca directed them to turn so they could see themselves in the mirror. "Not too bad, I must say."

Mark couldn't speak. It was as if he was with Becca McCleary in the summer of 1862.

"Are you okay?" asked Rebecca.

"Yes," he replied, his gaze still locked on their reflection.

Rebecca chuckled. "Well, we should probably go?"

"Yes, of course," he replied, finally breaking his focus from their reflection and turning to look into her inviting blue eyes.

The surreal feeling stuck with him as they made their way down the stairs.

"Isn't this cool?" asked Rebecca.

"This is … awesome."

"These balls can be so much fun," said Rebecca. "Just let yourself go and be in the moment. Before you know it, you'll think you've travelled back in time."

"I already feel like I have," he confessed.

At the bottom of the stairs he saw Clara.

She too was wearing period dress, except her dress was black with a white apron.

"Miss Becca," smiled Clara. "Mr. Patterson," she added with a bow. Carson is waiting to announce you to the room."

"Very well, Clara," said Rebecca, motioning for Mark to move toward the entrance to the main hall.

"She's okay playing—?"

"A slave?" interrupted Rebecca. "We don't think of it like that.   Clara and Carson know how important their family has been to us … for generations. They are part of this family … this land … this house."

Rebecca motioned for Mark to turn to his right. "Carson is standing at the entrance to the main hall. That is where you need to lead me."

"Yes, Becca," he said with a smile, caught up in the moment.

"I like that," replied Rebecca. "You should call me that for the rest of the night."

"Miss Becca—."

"McCleary," added Rebecca. "All the women of the family are McCleary tonight."

"Okay," he replied.

As they reached Carson, he gave a slight bow.

"We are ready," said Rebecca.

"Professor Mark Patterson of the New York Pattersons and Miss Rebecca McCleary!" boomed Carson as the already crowded room turned to watch them enter.

Mark was completely lost in the majesty of the ball. Dozens of people, in full period attire, filled the parlor and adjoining family room. The family room had been cleared to act as a dance floor and several couples were dancing to the period music. Behind the band was a massive South Carolina flag hanging from the vaulted ceiling.

"Wow," he mumbled.

"Do we know how to throw a party or what?" asked Rebecca.

"That you do, Rebecc—"

"Becca," she said with smile. "Don't forget."

"Miss Becca … of course."

"That's better," she replied, grabbing his arm. "Let's dance."

"I … uh … I don't know—"

"I'll show you," she said as Mark felt her pulling him toward the dance floor. "Just do what I say."

They rushed onto the dance floor and she turned back toward him, holding her arms in the air. "Put your hand here," she said moving her right hand for him to take.

He took her right hand with his left and held it

near her shoulder. "Like this?"

"Yes. Now put your other hand here," she continued, taking his right hand and placing it on the small of her back. "There ya go."

She stepped in close. The smell of her perfume reminded him of cotton candy.

"It's basically a waltz," she said as she moved to one side. "You lead."

Mark shifted his weight and after a few awkward steps was moving along with the music, pulling Rebecca around the dance floor.

"Not too shabby for a Yankee," said Rebecca.

"Hey. Yankees can dance too."

"We're about to find out," she replied as the tempo of the music increased and they began to move more quickly.

Before long they were almost bouncing around the dance floor in wide circles.

As they danced, he saw the curls in her hair bouncing and her cheeks grow flush.

Still bouncing and spinning around the room, he soon forgot about the steps of the dance; all of his focus was on her deep blue eyes.

She looked back, locking her gaze onto him.

Forgetting the world around them, the music had slowed for a few seconds before Mark realized it.

"Sorry," he said as a slow ballad continued to play.

"That's okay," she replied, catching her breath. "It's easy to get …" She looked up at him and stepped in close. "… swept away."

He felt her body against his as he pulled her even closer. "Yes. It is."

As the almost melancholy ballad played, Mark became even more lost in the sensations of the moment. The smell of her perfume, the oceans of blue that were her eyes, the silky gold hair, and … the pressure of her body against his.

"Do you know this song?" she asked.

"No. What is it about?"

"It's an old Scots-Irish song about at clan chief that gives up everything when he meets a Scottish farm girl on the road to York to marry an English noblewoman."

"I've never heard of it."

"It's about my one of my ancestors," she said with a smile. "It reminds us that you usually find love when you're least expecting it."

"That's a nice story," he said, still lost in her eyes.

"It's pretty hot in here," she said softly. "Maybe we should go for a walk out by the swamp."

"I don't know," he replied, a wave of guilt washing over him. Now he felt like he was cheating on Sarah by just the dance alone.

A frown came to her face. "C'mon, Mark. It's just a walk." She was almost pouting. "You did say you would be my escort, didn't you?"

"Okay," he said instinctively.

"Good," she replied with a smile.

Mark followed as Rebecca led him across the dance floor and to the exit at the back of the house.

"So how often does your family do this?" he asked as they strolled along the edge of the water.

"Every few years. Used to be annually when Nana was younger. I think I was thirteen or fourteen the first time I went to one. They are so fun … playing dress up and dancing."

"I've always wondered what it would be like to live in the South back then … And I feel a little like I'm doing that right now."

"Like you're with Becca?"

"Yeah …" He paused. "I'm sorry that's weird."

"No," replied Rebecca. "She kept this family alive. We are what we are because of her." She placed her hands in his. "Any one of us would be happy to be her."

"Her diary is so incredible."

"Do you want me to read from it?" she said. "I'm all dolled up like her. Would you like—"

"Yes!" he blurted. "Let me go get it."

"Oka—"

Before she could finish, he was off like a shot to retrieve the diary.

Mark ignored the party as he rushed through the house and to his room. Grabbing the diary, he opened it. Looking back at him was the picture of Becca. "Jesus," he said aloud. She really did look just like her. Closing the diary, he rushed back to Rebecca.

Bursting into the yard, he saw her sitting on a wicker bench by a small lamp that illuminated the path toward the swamp.

"That was quick," she said.

"Yeah …," he panted. "I … just …" He was so mesmerized he could barely talk.

"Here," said Rebecca, gently taking the diary from him with a chuckle. "You just sit there and listen."

Mark sat next to her.

"What do you want me to read?" she asked.

"Surprise me," he said.

"Okay … let me see … July 8, 1865. "*I met with Winthrop again today. Most of those carpetbaggers just want our land and look down on us. They think since we lost that they can lord over us like they are our masters. But not Winthrop. He said his grandfather was a Quaker and he didn't see any need to holding on to hate. He's not like any other Yankee I've ever met.*" She paused, looking up toward Mark. A coy smile formed on her face before she returned to the diary. "*I'm not sure daddy would approve, but since I'm the only McCleary left, I can decide if he calls on me. I think I'll let him. He's shy and serious.*" She looked up again. "*And always in his books but I can tell …*"

"What?" pleaded Mark. He hadn't read that far in the diary yet.

Even in the dim light she could see Rebecca blush.

"*… always in his books but I can tell he wants me.*" She glanced up at him and then back to the diary. "*I think I might be falling for a Yankee from New York.*"

Sweat began to form on Mark's forehead and he felt his heart pounding in his chest as Rebecca closed the book. "You picked a good passage," he said, looking into her blue eyes.

"I did?" she asked.

"Yeah," he mouthed.

He sensed her scooting closer to him and his pounding heart now began to race.

Her knee touched his and a jolt of excitement shot through his body.

"Call me Becca again," she whispered.

"Becca," he replied, leaning in toward her.

He felt her breath against his cheek.

"No," he blurted, sliding back away from her and standing.

"What?" she asked.

"I … I can't," he replied. "I …"

"Did I do something wrong?"

"No … no," he said. "I just …"

He looked down at her.

She was perfect. Beautiful. Inviting.

But she wasn't Sarah.

"I'm sorry. I shouldn't be out here," he said, more of a warning to himself than in response to Rebecca.

"Do you want to go back inside, Mark?"

"I …" It was all he could do not to pounce on her. He hated himself for it, but he had never been more attracted to a woman in his life.

But she wasn't Sarah.

"I think I need to call it a night."

"Are you sure?" She stood and stepped close to him. "The party just started."

Another whiff of her perfume hit him. He shook his head, fighting off the temptation.

"I'm sorry," he said as he turned and quickly returned to his room.

Making his way to his room, he removed his tailcoat and sat on the edge of his bed. He let his head fall into his hands.

His body still tingled from her touch and his gut was tight with guilt for enjoying it.

He stood, untucking the cotton undershirt. "Damn it," he cursed. He loved Sarah; he knew he did. But then why did Becc—Rebecca seem to draw him in like a moth to a flame? Every time he looked at her, his body felt more alive than the last time. How was—

There was a gentle knock at the door.

He knew who it was and that he shouldn't answer it.

Opening the door, he looked into those blue eyes again.

"Rebecca, I—"

"I just wanted to return this," she said, presenting the diary.

He'd completely forgotten about the diary. "Thank you."

"And I'm sorry," said Rebecca. "I was having so much fun … I just think …"

As he took the diary, his hand touched hers.

He looked down at her hand and then back into her eyes.

She closed her eyes and slowly opened them as he took the diary and broke contact with her hand. "I just think we got a little carried away in the moment."

"Yeah," he replied.

"But don't worry about it, Mark," she continued. "It was all just a bit of make-believe, right?"

"Right."

"Well, okay. I'll let you be … just wanted to get this back to you."

"Thanks," he said, offering a smile.

"Goodnight, Mark."

"Goodnight Becc—Rebecca," he said.

A partial smile came to her face before she turned and left to return to the party.

He slowly shut the door, leaning against it as it closed.

"Damn it."

***

"Fuck," cursed Rebecca, her body hot and frustrated, as she stormed down the hallway. Her thoughts elsewhere, she almost collided with Clara.

"Are you okay?" asked Clara.

"No," grumbled Rebecca. "I need to get out of here. I need to go out."

"But won't—" Clara stopped. Rebecca was already walking away. "Somebody's gonna have a bad night," she said to herself.

Chapter Six

Rebecca let her body slowly sway to the blue's song playing in the bar. Gripping the glass of scotch in her hand, she took a sip and looked around.

Her eyes met a tall, fit man in slacks and a silk shirt unbuttoned one button too many. He was attractive enough, with a strong jaw and short blond hair. Next to him stood what could have been his clone except for his brown hair and instead of a silk button-up, he wore a hundred-dollar polo shirt with the color 'popped' and a shell necklace draped over his neck. They both smiled.

'Frat boys or new money,' she thought to herself before smiling back at them.

She held their gaze long enough and then turned back toward the bar and took another drink. Looking over her glass, she saw them approaching her in the bar mirror.

"Hey, boys," she said, turning to greet them just as they reached her.

"Hello to you," said the man in the polo shirt, he eyes roaming over her body, well displayed in a tight black dress. "I haven't seen you here before."

"And you probably won't see me here again," she replied, finishing her drink.

"Looks like you need another drink, darling," said the man in the silk shirt, positioning himself on the opposite side of her from his friend, sandwiching her and moving closer.

Rebecca laughed. "What I need," she replied standing and letting her body rub against the man in the silk shirt while taking the other man's hand, "is to dance."

She drifted back out to the dance floor with both men close in tow. The band began to play a slow, sultry version of *Son of a Preacher Man* as she turned and smiled. "Well c'mon," she said, motioning with her finger.

As the female singer's gravelly voice began to sing the tune, the men moved around her. The polo-shirt man stepped in front of her as she felt the other press against her backside.

Rebecca raised her left hand to the cheek of the man in front of her as she slid her leg in between his, pushing against his groin. Her right hand reached back to grab the hair of the man behind her as he leaned in, his warm breath on her neck.

As the song played, she let them press up against her, grinding against her body as she slowly turned back and forth to catch the hungry gaze of each.

"I'm Michael."

"I don't care," replied Rebecca, running her hand down his torso.

She knew they were both aroused; she could feel it as they pressed against here. And their animal lust stirred her as well, the anticipation causing a tightness in her stomach.

It was time.

"Thanks," said Rebecca, sliding out from between the two men and walking back toward the bar.

Just as she reached the bar, she felt a hand grab her arm.

"What's going on?" asked the man in the silk shirt.

"I said I wanted to dance … and we danced," replied Rebecca with a smile.

"You can't just do that and walk away!" added the other man, his jaw tight with frustration.

"Do what?" she asked, feigning surprise.

"Get us all … you can't fucking tease us like that," huffed the man in the silk shirt, his grip tightening on her arm. "And I know you liked it," he said, leaning in close to her.

"Fine." Rebecca stood and raised a hand to each man's cheek, leaning between them. "If you want what I have, follow me."

Without looking to see their response, Rebecca stepped through them and walked toward the women's room as the band begins to play *Strangle Hold.*

***

The black and white video image from the bar's security camera showed Rebecca walking through the crowd with the two men behind her. Suddenly, the image shuddered, replaced by static.

***

Stepping inside bathroom, Rebecca turned toward a woman applying makeup at a mirror. "Get out."

The woman turns toward Rebecca and guffaws. "Bitch, you'd bett—"

"*Exeo,*" grumbled Rebecca, her voice

reverberating in a low echo as if more than one person was speaking.

The woman dropped her makeup brush and exited the restroom without emotion as the two men walked inside. The beat from the music was replaced by the words *'come on, come on, come up'* blasting into the room before the door shut, leaving only the reverberations of the music.

"Lock it," ordered Rebecca.

The man in the polo shirt smiled and complied.

Sidestepping as the men advanced, Rebecca positioned herself in front of the men as they stopped in front of an open stall.

With a devilish smile, she stepped toward the man in the silk shirt and kissed him hard, driving her tongue into his mouth. She then grabbed the other man's shirt and pulled him closer before shifting her mouth to his for a deep, passionate kiss.

As they kissed, she felt hands on her body including one that slide up the side of her leg, pulling her tight dress up toward her waist.

Rebecca directed the men into the stall and stepped away from her embrace but left a hand on each man's chest.

"Is this what you wanted boys?" she asked with a smile.

They nodded in agreement.

Rebecca slid her hands under the bottom of the man's polo shirt and started to pull it up. The man grabbed his shirt and continued to pull his shirt over his head. As he did, Rebecca shifted to the man in the silk shirt. "You too," she demanded as she placed her hands on each side of the row of buttons and pulled the shirt open. As buttons hit the tile floor, she leaned in a kissed the man's chest.

Her body tingled as she reached down and undid his buckle, grabbed his pants, and yanked them toward the ground.

Turning toward the other man, she moved his hands from his belt. "I'll take care of that," she said as she unlatched the buckle and pulled his pants down to his knees before running her hands up each man's bare torso. "Are you boys ready for the real magic?" she asked, dropping to her knees and sliding her hands down to each man's navel.

***

The man in the torn silk shirt glanced over at his buddy, still in disbelieve about what was happening. His friend smiled and nodded.

"Yes," said the men in unison as the man in the silk shirt look down to watch.

His body jerked as he looked into Rebecca's eyes. They were dark as coal.

***

"*Rigida!*" shouted Rebecca in that same deep, reverberating voice and the two men fell against the back wall of the stall.

The men's bodies began to spasm violently as Rebecca rose to her feet.

"Fucking trash," declared Rebecca. "You think you're worthy of this?" She leaned in toward the man in the silk shirt as he gasped for air. "What you're feeling is every muscle in your body seizing. Soon your lungs will collapse and your hearts will stop."

Giving each man a kiss on the cheek, she turned and walked to the mirror.

She slowly wiped a smudge of lipstick from her mouth and pulled her dress back down as she looked at the men in the reflection of the mirror.

They were dead.

She turned back toward the twisted and contorted corpses. "Thanks boys," she said, turning toward the exit. "I needed that."

***

Rebecca opened the main door to the McCleary House and softly walked through the foyer.

"Where have you been?"

Rebecca closed her eyes and took a deep breath before turning to greet her mother, who was sitting on an antique couch in the receiving parlor.

"I was out."

"You left right in the middle of the ball. And come back in that dress?"

"What's wrong with this dress?" asked Rebecca holding her arms out as if she was showing off a Sunday dress.

"And you called upon *him* tonight," snapped Brianna. "We *all* felt it."

"So," quipped Rebecca. "Isn't that why Becca McCleary called upon *him* in the first place, so that we could use *his* power?"

"When we need it, Daughter. Not when we want it."

"C'mon. I know enough about what happened here when I was a child to know that's not—"

Brianna rose from the couch.

Rebecca instinctively took a step back.

"You *must* respect him," warned Brianna.

"You think I don't, Mother?" replied Rebecca, her defiance returning. "I might be the only one that respects him enough to use his power the way it should be."

"And what way is that?"

"For whatever I want," said Rebecca with a smile. "Power is power, whether it's over a senator, a

CEO … or two pieces of trash from Daniel's Island."

"Rebecca, what did you—"

"Don't worry, mother. I know when—and how—to use what he has given me."

"I sometimes worry for this family when you become the matriarch," confessed Brianna, shaking her head.

Rebecca's jaw and her body tightened with anger—and his strength—welling up from deep inside her. "Who you should worry for, mother, is anyone that gets in my way." Her warning given, Rebecca relaxed, letting out a chuckle. "But none of this is why you're upset, Mother."

"Then please tell me, Rebecca. Why am I upset?"

Rebecca felt her skin grow flush, not from her mother's question but from her own frustrations with Mark. "I cannot press him. If I push too hard …" She paused. "And this fiancée … having to deal with this Yankee bitch isn't—"

"She is a problem that will have to be dealt with. All the more reason you can't allow—"

"I know what I'm doing," grumbled Rebecca. "Mark Patterson is mine, just like this family will be mine … and no one will prevent me from taking what is mine."

Chapter Seven

Mark anxiously waited for Sarah's Skype profile to open. He needed to talk to her—to see her. He needed to get his mind back on track … and to push the almost-constant thoughts of Rebecca from his mind.

The computer *beeped*, and Sarah's profile popped onto the screen.

He let out a sigh of relief when the camera focused on her face.

She was still in her uniform.

"So, are you ready to see me?" she asked.

"Oh, you have no idea," he replied.

"Well my flight gets in tomorrow afternoon."

"I got your email. It's all set up. A driver is going to pick you up and bring you straight here."

"You're not going to meet me there?"

"I promised Rebecca I would look over her grad school essay and if I do it first, I'll be done—"

"Rebecca?"

Why did he say that? And why hadn't it occurred to him Sarah would have wanted him to meet her at the airport? "She's just Mrs. Mackey's daughter.

She's a history major."

He could see a scowl forming on Sarah's face. "So, you're not meeting me at the airport. Because of a—"

"I can just tell her I can't do it. I … I just promised I would do this before I got your flight information and it took her longer to get it ready than she'd originally thought. The deadline's in a few days and—"

"Fine. Whatever," pouted Sarah. "I guess I better get used to co-eds coming after you."

Mark laughed, relieved Sarah appeared to be dropping the issue. "Yeah, right. I'm just looking over a paper. And I think I'll have to worry a lot more about senior partners than you will co-eds ... or tall captains when you're on your drill time."

He regretted the remark as soon as he said it.

"What?"

"Nothing. I was just—I just saw your beefy friend in the pics you sent."

"What, are you ... oh, John. Seriously? He's just another company commander. I'm pretty sure he just sees me as another one of the guys."

"I'm pretty sure he doesn't, not unless he's blind."

"It's not like ... you just don't ... I told you if you haven't been over there, then you don't understand. He's not ..." She stopped, looking up toward the ceiling. "Can we talk about something else? How's your dad?"

"I don't know." He stopped as a wave of emotion washed over him. "He says he's okay, but he looked thin in the last few pictures he's sent. I contacted his secretary yesterday and she said he was out for a few days on personal business. I think he's doing chemo again, but he won't tell anyone."

"I'm sorry. I know everyone thought he had it beat last time."

"Yeah. But it might not be that. I'm gonna be optimistic until I hear otherwise. Let's just focus on the fun stuff I've got planned for us when you get here."

"And what is that?"

"Maybe some horseback riding. A late-night boat ride. We can pick some wildflowers."

"Look at you, mister romantic. And you riding a horse … don't hurt yourself." She leaned in close to the screen. "How 'bout we just get that first night 'knocked out'," she said softly. "And we'll go from there."

"Works for me."

"Thought it would."

"I miss you," he said.

"I miss you too," replied Sarah, pressing her hand to the screen. "I gotta finish some paperwork then I'm gonna pack so I can get out of here and down there to you."

"See ya tomorrow, babe."

The Skype screen closed and Mark leaned back in his chair. 'Everything will be okay when she gets here,' he thought.

***

Mark stood beside Brianna at the foyer of the house as he waited for Sarah to arrive.

"Calm down, son," said Brianna with a smile. "She's your fiancée, not a new puppy. She'll be here soon."

"Sorry," he replied. "Just a little anxious." He needed her to be there.

The door began to open and his heart skipped a

beat.

His gaze fell on her as she entered the house.

She smiled. "Mark."

He returned her smile.

Suddenly the light in the foyer let out a 'pop' and went dark, followed by all of the lights in the center hallway.

Recovering from the surprise of the lights, Mark stepped forward and took Sarah in his arms. She squeezed him tight.

He had forgotten how strong she was. "I've missed you so much," he huffed, taking in a deep breath with her arms locked around him.

"Me too," replied Sarah.

"Mrs. Mackey," said Mark, turning toward Brianna. "This is Sarah Barkley. Sarah, this is Brianna Mackey. She was the one that gave me permission to do the research and for us to stay here."

"Nice to meet you, Mrs. Mackey," said Sarah, extending her hand.

"Welcome to the McCleary House, Miss. Barkley. Mark tells us you are a law student ... and a soldier?"

"Yes, ma'am," she replied with a glance toward Mark.

"Well, it's been a long time since we've had a Federal in our house." Brianna looked up to the burned-out lights. "Maybe the house still holds a grudge," she said with a smile.

Mark looked toward Sarah, who was staring blankly at Brianna.

"But we don't, honey," continued Brianna as she gave Sarah a hug.

"Well, both I, and the federal government, thank you," replied Sarah.

"Yes," said Brianna with a quick, dismissive chuckle. "I know you've had a long day of traveling so I'll let you get settled in. Mark knows our schedule by now, so he can keep you out of trouble."

"Thank you again."

"You're welcome. Have a good evening," said Brianna before walking toward the stairwell.

Mark embraced Sarah again. "We can get Thomas to …" Mark paused, noticing they were alone. "Where did he go?"

"I guess the *house* isn't the only one unhappy with a Federal here." Sarah turned back to Mark. "And who says 'Federal'? Did I get off the plane in 1863?"

"Maybe a little bit," said Mark with a chuckle. But—"

Mark stopped mid-sentence as Rebecca bounded into the hallway. She was wearing yoga pink pants and a black sports-bra that allowed most of her toned stomach to show.

"Hey, Mark. Thanks for reading my essay," she said before giving him a quick kiss on the cheek.

Mark could feel Sarah burning holes through his skull with her eyes.

"This has to be your fiancée," continued Rebecca. "He's talked so much about you. Sheri, right?"

"It's Sarah," replied Sarah with a forced smile. "And you just have to be Rebecca."

"The one and only. Guess Mark's mentioned me?"

"He's mentioned a few things," said Sarah, casting a frosty glance toward Mark.

"Cool. Well, I have to run. Gotta get my 5K in for the day. But I'm sure we'll talk a bunch in the next few weeks."

"Can't wait," said Sarah.

"Okay," said Rebecca with a slight tilt of her head toward Mark. "See you guys later," she added as she gave a little bounce before squeezing between Mark and Sarah on her way to the door.

Mark looked toward Sarah as the door closed behind Rebecca.

"You have got to be kidding me."

"What?" asked Mark.

"What? That is the history student you've been helping out? I'm as straight as they come and I ..." She grabbed his shirt and pulled him close. "You watch yourself with that one."

"C'mon, Sarah," he could feel sweat forming on his forehead. Was it that obvious?

"I'm not kidding, Mark. I can't believe that little thing's been bouncing around here for the last two weeks and you're worried about a picture I'm sending you?"

"She's just Mrs. Mackey's—"

"She isn't *just* anything, Mark. But that's okay. I'm here now and we're gonna shut Little Miss Perky Tits down."

Mark guffawed. "Sure. Can we just go upstairs?"

"As long as the *house* will let me."

"Very funny. I'll get your bags."

***

Mark sat at the desk in his room flipping through Becca McCleary's diary.

"So, every single husband?" asked Sarah through the bathroom door.

"Y ... Yeah," replied Mark, coughing slightly. "It's a little freaky. I mean there's absolutely no sign of foul play but yep ... every single one of them."

The sound of the bathroom door opening drew

his attention.

Sarah stepped out wearing a short plaid skirt and white button up shirt tied to show off her stomach and cleavage. Her hair was tied into two tightly-braided pigtails.

Mark coughed again.

"Well professor, I was wondering if I could get some extra credit."

Mark smiled. For the first time in days, Rebecca was the furthest thing from his mind. "Well, you do have a lot of work to make up for," he said.

Sarah stood over Mark, leaning forward so her breasts rested in front of his face. "I've been wanting to do this for weeks," she whispered as she kissed him on the neck.

Mark closed his eyes as a tingling sensation ran from his neck down his leg.

"Come here." Sarah rose to her feet, undoing the knot keeping her shirt closed. "You have some work to do," she added as she pulled him to his feet.

Mark's head was light as Sarah led him to the bed. It had only been two weeks, but his heart was racing like it was his first time.

Mark transitioned from light-headed to dizzy as Sarah turned him around and pushed him onto the bed. His mind spinning, he saw a large shadow pass across the wall toward the window. He closed his eyes and looked again but nothing was there. Mark coughed, closing his eyes and opening them again trying to gain his bearings.

"How 'bout we start off with an oral exam?" said Sarah as she crawled on top of him.

Mark groaned as she began to kiss his chest, slowly moving down his torso.

The pleasure of Sarah's tongue on his body

mixed with the dizziness and …

He began to cough forcefully.

"What's wrong?" asked Sarah, looking up toward him.

"Wh …" He coughed again. "What do you mean?"

"You've got a rash on …" She sat up on her knees. "Everywhere."

"I—" Another powerful cough interrupted him as he began to struggle to take in air.

"Mark?"

Mark let out a series of heavy coughs as Sara rose from the bed and poured him a cup of water.

Mark grabbed for the cup, but the first drink shot out of his mouth as he coughed again.

"Mark? Mark?"

He tried to answer but another wave of coughing stopped him.

"Here," said Sarah, sitting on the bed beside him and placing a pillow behind his back. "Do we need to take you to the ER?"

"I …" he coughed again, unable to answer.

"I'm gonna have someone call," said Sarah as she jumped from the bed and rushed out of the room.

***

Sarah rushed down the stairs, almost running into Rebecca.

"There's something wrong with Mark," panted Sarah. "He has a rash and is having trouble breathing."

"Is he okay?"

"No. He's not. We need to take him to the doctor."

"Okay," replied Rebecca. "I'll have Thomas bring the car."

"Hurry," said Sarah as she turned and rushed back to Mark.

Sarah bounded up the stairs, skipping most of the steps, and burst back into their room.

Mark was sitting on the edge of the bed. His complexion was returning to normal, his cough almost gone.

"Are you okay?

"I'm feeling much better. I don't want …"

Sarah ran her hand over Mark's face and chest, checking the rash.

"Really. I'm okay now."

"I still think we should take you to the ER."

"No. No," replied Mark. "I think I'm gonna be okay."

The sound of Rebecca rushing into the room drew Sarah's attention. "Thomas is bringing the car around." She looked at Mark. "Is he okay?"

"I'm okay. I just had a coughing spell. I don't need to go anywhere."

"It was a lot more than that," added Sarah, her anger growing. "It looked like were having trouble breathing. You should go in."

"Maybe it was just an allergic reaction. Happens a lot down here." Rebecca shifted her gaze from Mark to Sarah. "Or maybe it's just something different you've been exposed to."

Sarah returned Rebecca's stare but soon realized she was still wearing the schoolgirl outfit, with the white shirt open exposing her black bra. Her blood rushing to her face, Sarah turned away from Rebecca. "Well, I guess if you're not going to the hospital then everyone should just go back to what they were doing," she said, pulling the sides of her shirt together.

Rebecca smiled. "I'll have Clara run up some

Benadryl …" Rebecca paused. "… so that you can get back to, uh, what you were doing."

"Thanks," replied Sarah, "but we'll be okay now."

"Suit yourself," said Rebecca with a shrug of her shoulders. "But keep an eye on him," she added with a glance toward Mark. "You got a keeper there."

Sarah spun back around to face Rebecca. "I do. I do," she repeated, looking directly into Rebecca's eyes.

Mark felt an eternity pass as they two women started at each other for a few, very long seconds.

"Well, goodnight, ya'll," said Rebecca as she turned and walked out of the room.

As the door closed, Sarah turned back toward Mark. "Shit. That wasn't embarrassing at all."

"I'm …" He coughed lightly. "… sorry."

"Are you sure you're okay."

"I'll be okay."

"And it's not your fault," said Sarah as she kissed him on the forehead. "Let's just get some sleep."

***

Mark slowly opened his eyes.

He took a deep breath. Despite the coughing spell, his fiancée was with him and things should stay clear for him. And by clear, he hoped that his mind would be clear of thoughts of Rebecca.

He rolled over, but Sarah wasn't there.

His stomach sank. Was it all another dream?

"It's okay, sleepy. Just stay in bed."

Mark looked up to see Sarah exiting the bathroom. She was wearing a grey ARMY T-shirt and black running shorts.

"You feeling any better?" she asked as she began to stretch.

"I think so. That was weird."

"Yeah," replied Sarah. "Well this whole place is weird. And by place, I mean the South."

"Going for a run?" He didn't want to talk to her about the house … and definitely not about Rebecca.

"You're on the ball this morning. How do I look?" she asked, turning in a slow circle.

"You look—"

"Or maybe more like this?" interrupted Sarah as she pulled her shorts up tight to her hips and removed her shirt, showing her sports bra. "I just thought I'd bounce my tight ass around in the hot sun," she said in a fake Southern accent while she twirled her hair. She turned away from Mark and bent over, displaying her rear end to him. "Oh, mercy me. I hope I don't perspire."

"Funny."

"I thought so," said Sarah as she grabbed her shirt and pulled it over her shoulders. "Hopefully Miss Perky Tits—of the South Carolina Perky Tits—can keep her clothes on while I'm gone," she continued, still feigning a Southern accent.

"Now that's not fair. It *is* her house after all."

Sarah leaned in to Mark, placing her hands on his cheek.

She gave him a quick kiss. "She just needs to know that not *everything* in the house is hers," she said before giving him a playful slap on the cheek. "And so do you."

"Really?"

"Just watch your ass, Mark Patterson. I don't trust that little … that girl one bit."

"You don't have to worry about me," he replied. He hoped she couldn't tell he was trying to reassure himself of that.

"Bye, ya'll," said Sarah, stopping at the door for one more twirl of her hair.

As the door closed, Mark let his head fall back into the pillow. His emotions shifting between lust and guilt.

***

Sarah's muscles burned as she ran down the trail, but she liked the well it felt. She pushed herself harder as she kept pace with the beat of the music pounding on her in her ear. Each time she thought of Rebecca parading around Mark, she picked up her pace even more.

Soon she was sprinting.

Reaching a clearing, she slowed her pace then stopped.

Sarah closed her eyes and grimaced as a shot of pain ran up her leg.

She leaned over to rub her knee. As her hand ran over the scar tissue, her mind flashed to the explosion that caused the injury. She closed her eyes and the vacant face of Private Callahan as he lay in the sand came to her. "Fuck it," she cursed as she rose and took a deep breath.

Sarah burst into a sprint, intent on running out both her frustration with Mark and the memories of that horrible day in Afghanistan.

As she continued to run, the thoughts of Rebecca were replaced by the sounds and sights of combat as she focused on the path in front of her.

"Shit!" she said, sliding to a stop.

In front of her was rattlesnake. Pulling the earbuds from her ears, she sucked in much needed air. "Had to be a snake," she said as she looked to her left and then to her right before finding a large branch lying by the trail.

Picking up the branch, she raised it above her head.

Then she paused.

"It's your lucky day, buddy," she said as she slid the branch under the snake and giving it a jerk, sending the snake flying into the nearby brushes. "There ya go," she said, tossing the branch aside. "Better get some karma points for that shit."

The threat taken care of, Sarah returned to her run.

Sarah ran for nearly a mile before stopping again to take a quick break.

Placing her hands on her knees, she sucked in a few deep breaths before noticing a small hill to her left. The path ahead of her was flat for as far as she could see. "Boring," she huffed. Reaching down to rub her knee again, she could hear gunfire echoing in her mind. "Fuck it," she said as she left the path and started up the hill.

Pulling herself to the top of the hill, she pushed herself over a fallen tree and started down the opposite side. As she descended the hill, her speed increased. Pushing the knee pain from her mind, she shifted her weight quickly then leapt over rocks and fallen trees.

Leaping over another rock, her foot landed on wet leaves. She struggled to regain her balance but slipped and fell to the ground at the bottom of the opposite side of the hill.

"Shit," she cursed, pushing herself off the damp ground. Brushing the dirt and leaves from her body, an object on the ground caught her attention.

Kneeling down, she picked up an old brass button.

She examined it.

The letters "N.Y." were stamped on it.

"Mark will like this," she said as she slid the button into her pocket.

Sarah twisted her torso from side to side and hopped up and down a few times. "Here we go," she said as she turned up the volume of her music and started back up the hillside.

***

Back from her run, Sarah opened the door to the bedroom. "You're gonna—" The room was empty. "Mark?"

Noticing a piece of paper on the bed, she picked it up. It read: *Went to the U of C for a few hours. Hope you had a good run. Love ya!*

"Alright then … showering alone," she huffed as she pulled her shirt over her shoulders and walked into the bathroom.

In the bathroom, she pulled the button from her pocket and looked at it. "He'll probably be more excited to see you than me," she pouted before placing the button on the sink.

She turned on the water and placed her hand under the faucet. As the water began to warm, Sarah pulled the tab and water began to flow from the showerhead.

Sarah stepped out of her shorts and into the shower.

***

Rebecca, in a loose black dress and her hair down, sat on the floor of her room, an encircled pentagram drawn on the hardwood in front of her. In the center of the circle was a dead, desiccated spider.

"Fucking bitch," cursed Rebecca as she placed a knife to her hand and lightly ran it over her palm.

Grunting, Rebecca squeezed her hand, letting a

small trickle of blood drip from her fist onto the spider.

Looking up toward the ceiling, her eyes were black.

"*Hibere.*"

The spider jerked and came to life, scurrying under the door and into the hallway.

***

As Sarah began to shower, a spider appeared from behind the cabinet. The spider's legs began to move flitter up and down before it fell onto the sink.

Scurrying over the sink, the spider stopped by the button. Its long, hairy legs tapped up and down over the button. With a quick shake of a leg, the spider sent the button tumbling into the basin and into the drain.

The spider then made its way up the wall above the sink and toward the shower. At the shower, the spider crawled onto the shower bar above Sarah.

On the bar, it began moving its legs frantically.

Sarah turned off the water and pulled the curtain open, causing the spider to fall onto the ground.

Hitting the ground, the spider raised its front legs in the air, ready to strike.

Sarah's foot landed just an inch from the spider as she stepped from the shower onto the floor.

It leapt toward her foot but missed.

After a quick flutter of its legs, the spider scurried across the floor and under the door as Sarah closed it behind her.

As Sarah began toweling herself, the spider crawled up the dresser and into Sarah's clothes.

***

Mark opened the door to see Sarah sitting on the bed. "Sorry," he said. "I just wanted to—"

"Don't worry about it," interrupted Sarah. "But you might want to have our guests get an exterminator."

"What?"

Sarah pointed to the dresser.

Underneath a glass was the spider.

"Why didn't you kill it?" asked Mark with a scowl.

"My hero," guffawed Sarah. "I think it's a brown recluse."

"Then why didn't you kill it?" he asked again.

"Well, if I smash it then no one will be able to tell. If it is, they definitely need to have this whole house sprayed. It's a good thing I always check my clothes for crawlers."

"You do that?"

"You just need to wake up with a camel spider in your gear once and it instantly becomes habit," said Sarah, sliding the glass over a piece of paper and inverting it. "Here ya go," she said, extending the glass to Mark.

"I'll take your word on that," he replied, taking the glass but keeping it as far away from his body as possible.

"Oh, I almost forgot with all the excitement. I found a button for you while I was out running."

"A button?"

"Yeah, it's some old brass button. Figured it might be from the Civil War button. I know you like that stuff."

Mark's interest was piqued. "Really, did it have any markings?"

"Yeah, but I don't remember what they were," she said as she walked over to the sink. "It's an old button and I just thought ... Where the hell is it?"

"I'll help you look," replied Mark, still holding the spider at arm's length. He looked down at the spider as the its legs tabbed relentlessly at the glass prison. "After I take care of this."

***

Mark, Sarah, Carson, and Rebecca sat around the dinner table, examining the spider.

"Gross," said Rebecca, curling her nose.

"It's just a spider," replied Sarah, smirking. "But I think it could be poisonous."

"I think you're right, Miss Barkley," said Carson. "I'll have the exterminator out immediately."

The muffled sound of gunfire in the distance drew Mark's attention.

He looked toward Sarah. Her body was tight as she turned toward the sound of the gunfire.

"Where's that coming from?" asked Sarah.

"Oh. Our security teams use our range for practice every other Thursday," answered Carson.

"You have a range on your property?"

"Yeah," added Rebecca. "Wanna see it?"

Mark looked toward Sarah.

She had that look in her eyes.

"Yes," he replied.

Chapter Eight

"Here we are," said Rebecca over the rattle and crack of gunfire, stopping her car at the range.

Mark looked over the four men on the range as they fired at pop-up targets, occasionally shifting from their rifles to sidearms. All were tall and muscular, not unlike Sarah's 'friend' John. Each also sported a beard and multiple tattoos.

"It's our little O.K. Corral," continued Rebecca.

"This is the security team for your property?" asked Sarah, her brow furrowed.

"One of them," answered Rebecca as she opened the car door. "Follow me."

As they walked toward the men, the firing died down and one of the men turned toward them.

"Hey boys," said Rebecca with a wave. "We have some guests that wanted to come down and see you guys shoot."

The man looked back toward the others, who had also turned their attention to Mark and the women. They looked at one another and smiled.

"This is Mr. Miller," said Rebecca. "He's the leader of this team."

"Nice to meet you," said Mark.

"Yep," replied Miller.

"Can I shoot?" asked Rebecca.

The men looked at each other again, chuckling.

"You're the boss, Miss Mackey."

"Cool."

As Rebecca walked toward the firing line, two of the men blatantly stared at her behind as she walked past them, causing Sarah to snigger.

At the firing line, the fourth man handed a rifle to her. "Let me help you get set up," he said as he ran his hand down her side and placed the other on her shoulder.

"Jesus," murmured Sarah, shaking her head.

Mark felt his skin grow hot as he watched the man touch her. Then just a quickly he felt a wave of guilt wash over him for being jealous.

With the security guard's hands on her waist, Rebecca fired a shot from the rifle. It jarred her, knocking her back into the man's torso. She repositioned, fired again with the same result.

"That was fun," declared Rebecca.

"Yes, ma'am. It was," said the man who had been behind her with a smile.

"Thanks, boys," replied Rebecca, giving the man a wink that caused Mark's teeth to grind.

"Any time, Miss Mackey," replied the guard. "Anytime."

The guards gaze shifted from Rebecca to Sarah. "Wanna try?" he asked, extending the rifle.

Sarah glanced toward Mark and smiled. "Sure. I'll give it a shot."

Sarah walked over to the guard.

"Let me—"

"I think I got it," interrupted Sarah, taking the

rifle from the guard. Slinging the rifle over her shoulder, she grabbed a pistol and a magazine from the table. She shoved the magazine into the pistol and racked a round into the chamber before shoving it into her waist belt. "One of you boys wanna activate the course?"

The guard at the table looked toward Miller who responded with a shrug. "Fire it up."

Sarah winked at the guard. "You're a peach."

The first target activated and Sarah fired three rounds into it instantly. Another popped up and she checked off, recognizing it as an unarmed target. Two targets popped up several meters away and she quickly put rounds into both.

"Holy shit," mouthed Mark. He'd never seen her handle a weapon before and he couldn't tell if he was terrified or aroused.

Moving forward, Sarah let the rifle fall to her side by its sling and drew the pistol.

She pivoted and fired again, the metallic *clang* telling everyone she had again hit her target.

A few minutes later, a buzzer rang indicating the course sequence was over.

"Nice," said one of the guards, nodding in acknowledgment of Sarah's performance.

Returning to the table, Sarah removed the magazine from the rifle and verified the chamber was empty. "Clear," she said, setting the rifle on the table.

"Damn, girl," said the guard who had manhandled Rebecca. "Not too shabby."

"Would've been perfect except for that one civilian you hit," said another.

"That guy ..." replied Sarah as he handed the pistol, slide locked open, to the guard. "... he was a collaborator."

The men chuckled.

"Where did you serve?" asked Miller, extending his hand to her.

Sarah shook Miller's hand. Mark noticed her pause as she examined a tattoo on the man's forearm.

"A little time in Ghazni and a wonderful vacation in Helmand. You?"

Miller looked back toward the other men and then returned his gaze to Sarah. "Oh, here and there."

"I bet."

"So, you were in Helmand?"

"Yeah but I was just up there for admin support. You know, typical PowerPoint ranger, FOBBIT-type."

"Yeah," replied Miller.

Even Mark knew Miller didn't believe her.

Miller turned toward another guard and said something in what he thought was Arabic or Farsi.

Sarah's expression told Mark—and Miller—that she understood them.

"Well, guys," said Sarah. "Thanks for letting us pop off a few rounds."

"No problem," replied Miller. "Does your friend want to—"

"Oh no," answered Mark, waving his hands and shaking his head. "I'm a historian. Big fan of the 'pen is mightier than the sword' thing."

"Roger that," replied Miller, failing to hide a smirk.

"Can I shoot a few more times?" asked Rebecca.

"Whatever you want, ma'am," replied Miller, his gaze still on Sarah. "Didn't get your name?"

"Nope, you didn't," she replied with a smile.

As Rebecca walked toward the firing line again, she and Sarah exchanged fake smiles.

By the time Sarah reached Mark, Rebecca had started to fire the rifle again. As the other men watched Rebecca shoot, Miller turned back to look at Sarah.

"That was awesome—" Mark felt Sarah grab his hand as she turned her back to the others.

"What the fuck is this family into, Mark?"

"What do mean?"

"Those guys aren't some fat, retired cops in golf carts. And they aren't fucking cheap."

"What are you talking about?"

"Those guys are straight up meat eaters."

"What?"

"Operators."

Mark let out a frustrated grunt. "I don't know what you are saying," he confessed. "Stop speaking Army."

Sarah returned the grunt. "Special operations. One of those guys is a SEAL, the other is DELTA. I'm guessing all of them are SOCOM."

Mark knew enough to understand those terms.

"I don't know. I mean the family has a lot of money. So, I guess they just want good—"

"These guys aren't good; they're the best. And people don't hire them because they can. You buy these guys because you need them."

Mark saw Miller still looking at them over Sarah's shoulder.

"I can ask—"

Her grip on his hand tightened.

"Don't. Jesus, Mark. These are not the kind of guys you ask questions. Whatever they are here for, just be glad you don't know about it."

"Don't you think you're being just a little—?"

"Goddamn it, Mark. These are the type of guys

who'll stick a knife in your neck and watch you bleed out with less thought than you give to honking your horn at a shitty driver on the freeway."

"Fine. But what was all that talk about where you'd been?"

"Just soldier stuff. They wanted to know if I'd seen any action."

"Why didn't you just tell them?"

"Those guys don't need to know shit about me. Let's just get back to the house and keep the fuck away from these guys."

Mark still didn't understand Sarah's apprehension about being around the men, but knew she was serious. "No problem with me. You're the one that wanted to come out here."

"Yeah, I did. And now I want to leave."

***

Sarah was on edge all day and halfway through dinner she still hadn't said a word.

"How do you like the pheasant, Miss Barkley?" asked Brianna, forcing Sarah to finally speak.

"It's fine, Mrs. Mackey. I just don't have much of an appetite today."

"I'm surprised," added Rebecca. "The way you were shooting, I would have worked up a big appetite if I was you."

"Shooting?" asked Brianna.

"Oh, yes," replied Rebecca. "They wanted to go to the range, so I took them down and we shot a bit with the boys."

"I see," said Brianna. "How was it?"

"I was fine," replied Sarah. "Thanks for taking us," she continued, looking toward Rebecca and painting a smile on her face.

"I guess being a soldier, you are used to guns,"

posited Brianna.

"Used to …" said Rebecca again, glancing toward Sarah, "… she was good." She paused, shifting her gaze to her mother. "Really good."

"Well," replied Brianna. "I guess—"

"Did you ever shoot anyone?" blurted Rebecca. "I bet you did."

Mark turned to Sarah. Her mouth was gaped, trying to formulate an answer she didn't want to give.

"Sarah is a combat veteran," said Mark as he placed his hand on her knee under the table. "We should probably leave it at that."

"I didn't mean to … I just assumed you get asked that a lot once people find out—"

"I do," replied Sarah.

"I think we should drop the topic," said Brianna. "And let Miss Barkley finisher her dinner in peace."

"Thank you, Mrs. Mackey," replied Sarah. "But if I may be excused?"

"Of course, dear," said Brianna.

"Thank you, everyone, for a wonderful dinner," said Sarah as she rose from the table and exited the room.

Mark began to stand. "If you'll—"

"Yes, of course," interrupted Brianna.

"Ladies," he added as he stood and followed Sarah upstairs.

He caught up to her just as she was entering their room and stepped in behind her.

As soon as the door closed, Sarah turned and took Mark's hand in hers.

"We need to leave this place."

"C'mon, Sarah. You're overreacting. I'm sure she just doesn't know not to ask a question like that—"

"It's not about the fucking question, Mark. And

I'm not overreacting. You can't tell me there's not something bad going on here."

"Because of those guards?"

"I just got a bad feeling about all of this. A feeling I haven't had since I was over there."

"Are you sure you're just not transferring—"

"Don't start that psychological bullshit with me, Mark. I know what that place did to me. And you don't understand what it means when people like that are around."

"You seemed to get along with them pretty easily."

"Yeah," she chortled, "too much. And I shouldn't have told them as much as I did."

"What are you talking about?" Mark grew even more frustrated. He never knew how to deal with Sarah when she started down this dark path. "I'm just trying to get my dissertation done and spend some time with you."

Sarah directed him to sit on the edge of the bed.

As he sat, she knelt in front of him, taking his hands in hers. "I know I haven't talked a lot about what I did over there."

"You were an interpreter for the military police?"

"At first. After ... after the first time I was injured I started working with a group that carried out raids against high value targets."

"What?"

"They needed women that spoke the language and had combat experience. I worked with guys like those we saw today. I know what they are capable of, Mark. The things they ..." She stopped, taking a deep breath. "... *we* did over there ..." She shook her head as if trying to wash away a memory. "Whatever this family is hiding, they are employing people that are more than capable, and even more willing, to kill to keep it hidden."

Tears formed in her eyes as she continued. She had rarely allowed herself to be so raw … so vulnerable.

He pulled her up to him. There was no way he could refuse her. "I'll tell them tomorrow that we'll leave after the weekend."

"Really?"

"We can move into Charleston this weekend and I'll just drive in to look at their records."

"Thank you," she said, kissing him.

She kissed him again.

Her kisses grew more passionate and Mark scooted back on the bed as she lay on top of him.

A loud knock on the door broke their embrace.

"Mark!" came Rebecca's voice from the other side. "Are you busy? I'm sorry to interrupt but I need to talk to you."

Mark felt the pressure of Sarah's body lessen as she rolled off him and onto her back.

"Seriously?" she huffed, staring at the ceiling. "Well, go ahead and open the fucking door."

"I'll just tell her we're busy."

"For fuck's sake just open the damn door."

Mark slowly rose from the bed and opened the door.

"I'm so sorry to bother …" Rebecca looked toward Sarah. "… you two. Hi, Sarah."

Sarah waved, a frustrated smirk chiseled on her face.

"I'm really sorry. I can—"

"Go ahead, Rebecca. What is it?" huffed Sarah.

"Mark, I hate to do this, but I just found out

UNC needs a sample of my work submitted with my admissions package and it needs to go out tomorrow. I really don't want to bother you this late but is there any way you can go over this with me tonight?"

Mark glanced back toward Sarah.

"Fine. Whatever," conceded Sarah, rising from the bed and walking toward the bathroom. At the door she stopped. "This weekend, Mark," she added before slamming the bathroom door.

***

Lying alone in bed while Mark was with Rebecca, Sarah fumed. Rolling over repetitively, smashed her pillow with her fist several times before finally settling onto her back.

"Bullshit," she mumbled to herself a she stared at the ceiling.

Eventually, she slowly drifted off.

In her subconscious mind, she heard the muffled sound of gunfire.

The muffled gunfire erupted into an explosion of noise as Sarah crawled from the wreckage of a Humvee.

Crawling free of the mangled vehicle, she turned to look at her knee as blood began to seep through her uniform.

She turned to her right as a private dove for cover beside her.

"You okay, LT?" he asked.

"Callahan" she grunted. "I'm okay. Just ... damn it," she cursed as the pain began to radiate from her leg. "Just—"

Rounds impacted above her head.

Turning toward her right, she raised her rifle and fired a burst as two Taliban fighters rushed her position. The combined fire of Sarah and the private sent their attackers tumbling to the ground.

"We gotta get clear of this vehicle, ma'am!" shouted Callahan as he grabbed her and began to drag her toward a nearby ditch.

Sarah looked up just as a round slammed into the private's helmet with a thud.

She fell to the ground as his body slumped and collapsed on top of her. Letting out a loud grunt, Sarah pushed the body of the private off her onto the sand.

"Callahan!" she shouted as she looked at the private. Blood was already flowing freely from his helmet and she could see grey matter stuck to the inside wall.

"Shit!" she cursed, looking into his vacant eyes.

Sensing movement, she turned and let out a scream as she fired point blank into the chest of an on-rushing Taliban fighter.

As he fell, another Taliban leapt on top of her.

The sweat-coated skin and stink of his breath filled her senses and she struggled to direct his knife away from her. With a grunt, she reached up and bit down hard on his cheek. Her mouth filled with sweat and blood as she grabbed the knife in her vest.

Pulling the knife from her vest, she pressed her back into the sand as she arched her body and drove the knife into his neck.

The thick, warm shower of blood coated her face and she let out a primal scream.

Sarah awoke screaming.

Sitting up in the bed, she took repetitive deep breaths to calm herself as she pulled her knees to her chest. She was soaked in sweat and her head pounded.

She looked toward the other side of the bed. Mark was still gone.

After a final deep breath, she looked toward a bottle of pills on the nightstand.

***

"What was that?" asked Mark, hearing Sarah's screams from the other side of the house.

"Probably just an old screech owl," replied Rebecca. "They'll scare the pants off you the first time you hear it."

"Okay," he replied, turning his attention back to her paper. "I've got to tell you, Rebecca, this is a really strong paper. Good research, good conclusions, and really good insights."

"You're just saying that," she replied, placing her hand on his shoulder.

"No … it's really good. You'd to make a great historian … if you weren't going to be running a multibillion-dollar corporation someday."

"Maybe I'll just give it up and become a stodgy history professor," she said, running her hand from his shoulder down his arm. "Maybe I'll work with you some day."

"That would be nice," he replied with a smile.

***

Brianna Mackey looked up from her desk in the dimly lit study as Clara entered the room.

"Mrs. Mackey," said Clara. "Mr. Miller is here as you requested."

"Send him in, Clara," she replied with a slight sigh.

"Mrs. Mackey," said Miller as he strode into the room, stopping in front of Brianna's desk. He wore black tactical pants and a tight, tan shirt with short, camouflage sleeves. His right hand, resting next to a holstered .45 caliber pistol, held a manila folder.

"Is that it?" she asked.

"Yes, ma'am," he replied reaching the folder to her. "That's what information we could get on her on short notice … but it's enough."

Brianna looked at white label on the folder, titled Sarah Barkley, Captain, USA.

She opened the folder to see a photo of Sarah in dress uniform, adorned with rows of medals, badges, and ribbons. "Hmm," she said softly, flipping through the documents.

"I knew there was something up at the range, so I started making some calls, anticipating you'd be interested," said Miller.

"I am," said Brianna, her gaze still on the documents in front of her.

"Two combat tours, Purple Heart times two, Silver Star …"

"So, she's a soldier." Brianna looked up from her desk.

Miller sat in a leather chair near a tall book case. "She's a little more than that, ma'am. You'll see she's also fluent in Farsi, an expert in small arms and close quarters combat … and in advanced interrogation techniques."

"Interrogation? She sounds like a female version of you," she laughed, concealing a growing concern.

"She pretty much is, ma'am."

Brianna let out another chuckle.

Miller leaned forward. "I'm serious, ma'am. Like I said, I made some calls."

"How does a woman get a record like this?"

"You do what you need to in order to win … so that's how it started."

"Explain."

"We often went after high-value targets that had wives and daughters. Sometimes word came down that they were to be interrogated, too. But they needed women to do it effectively.”

“I see.”

“So, they took a few hundred women with combat experience and had them go through screening to work in special operations. Ten or so made it through the training.”

“Ten?” Brianna’s stomach tightened.

“One of my guys said she’d worked with DELTA when he was in Helmond.”

Brianna, focusing on Miller’s words, shifted slowly through the documents.

She stopped on one marked ‘medical records’.

“Clonidine … for—”

Miller laughed. “Half your security pops it like candy.” He paused, leaning back in the chair. “What gets me is … I just don’t know what the hell a woman like that is doing with that guy?”

“What do you mean?”

“He might be rich but … I dunno, it’s just …” He shook his head. “It’s like a lion shacking up with, hell … something a lion eats.”

“You do have a way with words, Mr. Miller,” replied Brianna.

“You don’t pay me to talk pretty, ma’am,” he replied with a smile.

“True,” said Brianna. “So, what does all of this mean?”

“She’s basically seen and probably done most of the shit the guys on my team have.”

Brianna closed the folder. “Would she know about what you and your security teams do for us?”

“Probably nothing specific … but she damn sure knows what *type* of things we do.”

Brianna exhaled heavily. “Then tell me, Mr.

Miller. What am I supposed to do about her?"

Miller stood. "Well, Mrs. Mackey. If she's going to be around your family I'd say you have two options."

"And those are?"

Miller smiled. "Hire her … or kill her."

Brianna leaned back in her chair. "I don't believe we have any positions available at this time."

"We can take care of it tonight, if you'd—"

"No," interrupted Brianna. "Not just yet. I need to watch her for a while. She could turn out to be useful to us," she added as she stood and began to unbutton her shirt. "And you have other things to take of right now."

Brianna removed her shirt and watched as Miller slowly made his way around the desk. As he reached her, she pulled her skirt to her waist and slid her behind onto the desk.

"I really like your company's benefits," said Miller as he removed his shirt. "I—"

"Remember, I don't pay you to talk," interrupted Brianna, pointing toward the floor.

Miller smiled and dropped to his knees. "Yes, ma'am."

***

Sarah made her way down the stairs and through the kitchen toward the back. The pills weren't working and with Mark fawning over his little Southern peach, she need some air. Stepping outside onto a small elevated deck, she inhaled heavily and then forced out a quick puff of air.

"Trouble sleepin?"

"Fuck," cursed Sarah, startled by the unexpected voice.

Looking down over the deck she saw Miller.

"Sorry to scare you," he said as he stepped into the light.

"I'm fine," she said bluntly.

"These warm nights are the toughest," continued Miller, walking up the two steps to the deck. "It's more humid than over there, but not as hot," he said, pulling a can of beer from pack and offering it to her.

Sarah stood motionless.

"C'mon," said Miller, still offering the beer.

She sighed and took the can, opening it. "Yeah."

"About the heat or trouble sleeping?" asked Miller, now leaning against the railing next to Sarah.

She took a drink. "Both."

Miller took another drink as well.

"That was some nice shooting today."

"Lucky day," she said.

He turned toward her. "I don't think that was luck."

She finished the beer and tossed it from the deck before turning to face Miller. "Maybe it wasn't," she replied, staring straight into his eyes.

"I didn't think so."

"I'm guessing you know—"

"Davidson from DELTA works for Mrs. Mackey also."

Sarah nodded. They definitely knew about her if they had talked to Davidson. "Figured one of his ex-wives would have killed him by now."

Miller laughed. "He probably deserves it," said Miller, handing her another beer.

She took the beer and opened it. "We all deserve it."

"That we do, Captain."

Sarah poured the rest of the can down her throat.

She'd had enough of the small talk.

"Look, man. I'm done with all of that shit," she said, tossing the second can into the darkness. "And I don't care, don't know, and don't want anything to do with whatever is going on here."

"That's good," replied Miller, stepping closer to her. "Because my employer gets a little nervous about having someone who tortures and kills women and children living under her roof."

Sarah stood her ground. "Then how do you explain yourself?"

"I don't live under their roof," he replied. "And from what I hear, you could give me a run for my money in that department."

"Well, your employer will be happy to know I'm out of here tomorrow," said Sarah.

"I'm sure she'll be happy to hear that."

"She's not the only one," added Sarah.

"Another one?" asked Miller, tossing another beer to Sarah.

Seeing half the beers already gone, she knew he wasn't on duty. "What are you doing out here so late?" she asked.

"Oh, my employer can be pretty demanding sometimes," he answered, his mouth twisted in a telling smile.

"Well, best of luck to ya," she said, refusing the beer and turning toward the entrance.

"Hey, captain?" asked Miller as Sarah started to walk away.

"What is it?"

He walked up close to her again, looking over her body.

"I gotta ask?"

"What?" she huffed.

"What in the hell are you doing with that academic dandy? There's no way that guy can take care of what you need."

Sarah smiled. "I figured I'd upgrade from brainless trigger pullers that play with guns to make up for their small dicks."

Miller shook his head slowly and raised his beer in the air as Sarah turned and walked away. "Well you got a nice six there, captain," he said as she entered the house.

The door closed behind her and he took another drink from his beer. "You better fucking watch it."

Chapter Nine

Mark stared at Sarah as she took a long drink from her Mai Tai.

When he had returned from helping Rebecca the night before, she'd just rolled over and ignored him and things hadn't gotten much better as the day went on.

"How many more of those are you going to have?" he asked.

"I don't know. How much longer do we have to stay here?" answered Sarah before taking another drink.

"Just a bit," replied Mark. "When I told Brianna this morning that we thought it would be better if we stayed in Charleston, she wanted to have a barbeque before we left. I thought it would be rude to say no."

Sarah took another drink. "How very Southern of them."

Mark turned toward Clara as she walked up to the table. She always seemed to surprise—and unnerve him.

"More Mai Tais, Ms. Barkley?" asked Clara.

"Fill'er up," answered Sarah, extending her class.

"Just let me know if you need anything else?"

replied Clara as she filled Sarah's glass.

"Sure will," said Sarah, throwing the drink back. "Let's top it off again."

Clara glanced at Mark.

"I don't need his permission," snapped Sarah.

"Of course, ma'am," complied Clara, refilling Sarah's glass again.

As Clara walked away, Sarah leaned in toward Mark. "I don't know what they're putting in these Mai Tais, but they're fuckin' awesome." Sarah's gaze shifted over Mark's shoulder. "Fucking great ... perky tits incoming at six o'clock."

Sarah raised her drink toward Rebecca as she approached. "Hi there, Becky."

Rebecca paused, clearly bothered by being called Becky. Quickly regaining her composure, she sat down next to Mark.

He could feel the hatred radiating off Sarah as she spoke.

"Hopefully Mark was able to help you with your homework last night."

"He was very helpful," said Rebecca, casting a smile toward Mark before returning her gaze to Sarah. "Thanks for letting me borrow him last night."

Sarah emptied her drink. "Yep."

"Well, I'll let you two be. Oh, and I'm sorry to hear you'll be staying in Charleston." Rebecca looked toward Mark. "But I'm sure we'll bump into each other while you're here looking at the family papers." She then turned toward Sarah. "I guess we probably won't be seeing much more of you out here though."

"Probably not."

"That's a shame," replied Rebecca with a wide smile. "See you later, Mark," she added, standing to leave.

Mark stood as she did, having grown accustomed to Southern practice.

As Rebecca walked away, Sarah stood as well. "Come with me," she said, taking Mark's hand.

"Where are we going?"

"We're going for a walk. You're gonna fuck me on that bitch's property at least once before we leave."

***

"This will do," said Sarah as she pulled Mark toward her as she leaned against a tall willow tree.

She kissed him hard.

Mark returned her kiss and felt her unbutton his pants. He let out a moan as she grabbed him.

She was not wasting any time on foreplay.

"Just slide them out of the way," she whispered as she wrapped her left leg around his waist.

Mark ran his hand up her dress and pulled her panties to one side.

"Do it," she huffed.

He let out a grunt as he pushed inside her.

Sarah let out a low moan. "I've been waiting a long time for this." Mark looked into her alcohol-glazed eyes as she stared at him. "Fuck me," she ordered.

Mark began to thrust faster.

"Faster," panted Sarah.

As he began to push himself into her more forcefully, he noticed something in the distance over Sarah's shoulder.

He saw someone.

It was Rebecca. Watching them.

He paused momentarily.

"Harder," demanded Sarah, wrapped a hand around his neck and pulling him toward her.

He obliged.

He looked back over her shoulder, sure he had imagined seeing Rebecca.

She was there.

As he continued to thrust into Sarah, his eyes locked onto Rebecca.

Rebecca pulled her skirt to her waist. She ran her hand over her stomach and then under her panties.

Unable to look away from Rebecca, he began to spasm as Sarah moaned.

"Mark," she groaned.

"Becca," he replied.

A guttural scream broke his gaze and he looked toward Sarah just as a cottonmouth snake from a nearby limb sank its fangs into her neck.

Sarah's body tightened as the snake fell to the ground. The snake hit the ground and struck again, biting her leg.

As Sarah fell to the ground, Mark glanced back toward Rebecca.

She was gone.

"Are you okay?" he asked, turning his attention back to Sarah.

"No," she grunted. "I need … I … I …"

"Sarah!" he shouted as she lost consciousness.

***

Mark sat in the waiting room with Thomas, leaning forward with his head in his hands. His stomach churned and his heart pounded. Was it his fault? Did he really see Rebecca watching them? Why was he thinking about Rebecca at all with his fiancée in the emergency room? As he searched for more ways to blame himself, Rebecca and Brianna rushed into the waiting room.

Mark didn't react; he was lost in guilt.

"We got here as quickly as we could. How is

135

she?" asked Rebecca.

Mark looked up, staring at her blankly.

"Mr. Patterson."

Mark turned away from Rebecca to see a doctor standing above him.

"That's me," he replied as he stood. "How is she?"

"Well it seems like she took a pretty big dose of venom from those two bites, but she should be okay."

"Thank God. Can I see her?"

"She's sleeping now and will be out of it for a day or so. We'll keep her for a few more hours and let her go if she has someplace where she can rest and someone to watch her."

Rebecca put her hand on Mark's shoulder. "She does."

Mark spun around. His blood boiled. "Can we talk?"

"Of course."

Mark led Rebecca away from the others. Once they were out of sight, he pressed her against the wall. "I need you to stop."

"Stop what?" she gasped, trying to get free from his grip.

"You know what I'm talking about. You're a beautiful woman but I'm engaged. You just need to leave me alone. I—"

"Leave you alone? What are you talking about?"

"Stop it, Goddamn it. I saw you there, watching us. You were ... touching yourself. It's—"

"What the hell are you talking about?"

"When Sarah and I were in the woods before she was bitten, I saw you watching."

"You're still drunk," declared Rebecca. "You don't know what you're saying."

"Maybe I am. But I know what I saw."

"I don't know what you think you saw but that is disgusting. I was with my family the whole time. I can't believe—"

"I know you're trying to seduce me but—"

The sting of Rebecca's hand slapping him stopped him mid-sentence.

"That's for being an asshole. All I've done is be nice to you and Sarah. And to have you … I know it's been a rough day so I'm not going to tell Mother about this. If I did, that would be the last you'd see of our records and your fiancée would have to lie in some hotel bed to recover instead of under the care of a nurse we could provide."

Mark released his hold on her and Rebecca stepped past him only to turn to face him again. "Son of a bitch," she cursed.

Now it was her that shoved him against the wall.

She moved in close, pressing her body against his. "And be assured, Mr. Patterson …"

He felt her body against him and the warmth of her breath on his neck as she leaned in close to him. "If I was trying to seduce you, I would have already had you."

***

Rebecca stormed away from Mark and through the waiting room.

"Let's go, Mother," she grumbled.

As Brianna joined her and they exited the hospital, Rebecca's pace slowed and a bounce returned to her step.

A few feet away was Carson, waiting next to the open door of a black SUV.

"Thank you, Carson," said Brianna, sliding inside.

"Take us home," ordered Rebecca as she joined her mother.

"Yes, ma'am," replied Carson, closing the door.

"Why are we leaving?" asked Brianna as the SUV pulled away from the hospital entrance.

"I did what I came to do," she huffed.

"And what exactly was that?"

"Just show him I was concerned," replied Rebecca. "He's still fighting ..." She paused. "That fucking Yankee skank has sunk her fangs deep into him, so it will take time to pry them out."

Brianna turned her body toward Rebecca, her jaw tight. "Just remember, we don't have forever, dear." Her mouth curled into a smile. "Perhaps you should try—"

Rebecca laughed, raising her hand to silence her mother. "You weren't really just going to tell me how to take a man from another woman, were you?" She turned away, looking toward the front of the vehicle. "Trust me. I don't need a lesson from—"

"Well if you don't take him from her," scoffed Brianna, "you could ruin us all and you'll end up spreading your legs for some lawyer or accountant South of Broad just to have a place to live."

Anger bubbled under Rebecca's skin. "Who I'm spreading my legs for is none of your business," she snapped.

"It is," grumbled Brianna. "And more importantly it is *his* until you get rid of this Yankee bitch and bed Mark."

"Bed," laughed Rebecca. "You mean fuck, Mother. Until I fuck him."

"Why do you have to be so crass?"

Rebecca leaned in toward her mother. "Because I can. Because no one will stop me. Because it upsets you so. You tell me I'll have to whore myself out for a place to live if I fail but don't like it when I say 'fuck'? What's wrong, Mother? Jealous you were only bedded by your husband and never *fucked*? Is that why you pay the help to do it?"

***

Brianna raised her hand to slap her insolent daughter.

But she couldn't move it.

"Stop it!" demanded Brianna as she looked into her daughter's now coal-black eyes.

"Say please," reverberated a low gravelly voice from Rebecca's mouth.

Brianna gnashed her teeth before grunting, "please."

"Okay," replied Rebecca, her voice now normal, before releasing mental control of her mother's arm.

Brianna sat back against the seat of the SUV and ran her hands over her legs, calming herself. "You understand, Rebecca, that we all had that same rush of power when it was our time?"

***

Rebecca smiled. "That makes sense," she said matter-of-factly. Her gaze shifted to the reflection of Carson's eyes in the rear-view mirror. "But given Carson and Clara telling me I'm the closest thing to Becca McCleary herself they've ever seen ..." She turned back toward her mother. "I'd say I'm special to *him*."

Rebecca's attention was drawn to a BMW as it sped past them and cut into their lane, causing Carson to brake.

She closed her eyes and opened them, her mind now linked to the BMW's driver. "*Occaeco*," she said softly in Latin.

The BMW swerved and then drifted into oncoming traffic, slamming head-on into a utility truck in a horrific explosion of metal.

"See," said Rebecca as her guffawed. "Special."

"And why must you use Latin?" asked her mother, more concerned about her daughter's language than the people she had just killed.

"Because it sounds better than that swamp gibberish," she replied. "And *he* doesn't seem to mind if I use it. So, you just stop worrying about me and what I am going to do about that Yankee *cunt*," she added, giving emphasis to the most offensive word she could think to say to her mother.

Chapter Ten

Mark stood outside of Sarah's room talking to one of the nurses hired by Brianna Mackey.

"How is she today?" he asked.

"She's still heavily sedated, sir," replied the nurse in a deep Carolina accent.

"I know. I tried to talk to her this morning, but she seemed to be in and out of consciousness. But ... how is she?"

"The grogginess is to be expected," said the nurse.

"But it's been two days already. Shouldn't there be some improvement?"

"Don't expect too much yet," replied the nurse with a reassuring smile. "She needs to rest. Remember that's why you brought her back here and gave her a room to herself. It's also why Mrs. Mackey hired me to watch her for the next few days." She placed her hand on Mark's arm. "Just give her some time and she'll be back up and around before you know it."

"Can I see her?"

The nurse exhaled heavily. "I guess it would be okay. Just make it quick."

"Thank you," replied Mark, turning from her and opening the door.

He was immediately overcome with a mixture of guilt and pity.

Sarah lay in the bed, shivering. Her skin was pale and covered with dots of perspiration. Even semi-conscious, her breathing was labored to the point of panting.

"Sarah?"

Her only response was what appeared to be a painful spasm.

He could tell she was still not in any condition to talk. Kneeling by the bed, he placed his hand on her forehead. It felt so hot.

"I'm so sorry, Sarah. The nurse says you should be doing better in a few days."

Her eyes slowly opened and she reached for him.

"Get … me … out …" She trailed off.

"Soon, babe. Just rest," he replied, kissing her cheek.

She was unconscious again.

"I'll let you get some more sleep."

He kissed her forehead and rose to his feet.

With a sigh, he turned and left the room.

***

Sarah forced her eyes open.

Her head ached and every muscle in her body spasmed. Through the pain, she struggled to focus her thoughts.

Panting, she closed her eyes, and with all her strength, rolled herself onto the ground. Hitting the floor with a thud, she groaned, pain exploding from every joint. The room grew cloudy and she lost consciousness.

Moments later, Sarah slowly opened her eyes

again.

Her mind flashed to her crawling toward cover after pushing the Taliban attacker off her body. If she made it through that, she could do this. She rolled to her side, letting out a feeble groan, spent from the exertion. Her face rested on the floor and her eyes slowly focused on the features of the wood as she took in heavy breaths.

Slowly, her gaze shifted further away, underneath her bed.

From her vantage, she could see a small burlap bag lying in the center of the floor under the bed. Grunting through the pain, she dragged herself closer.

Taking another minute to muster the strength, she swung her arm under the bed and grabbed the satchel.

Slowly pulling the satchel across the floor, she shifted her hand to the bottom of the bag and with a few jerks, emptied its contents onto the floor.

Inside was a mixture of small bones, roots, and the half-decayed internal organ of some small animal.

As she examined the morbid contents, her vision grew clearer and the spasm of her muscles lessened.

The pain continued to subside and Sarah pushed herself to her hands and knees. Still breathing heavily, she pulled herself to the edge of bed and raised up to her knees. Leaning on the mattress, her mind flashed back to something else she had seen while lying on the floor.

Sarah summoned her restored strength and shoved the mattress off the bed with a grunt. Still not fully recovered, however, she stumbled as the mattress slid onto the floor but grabbed the bedframe in time to balance herself.

"What the fuck?" she mouthed.

Under the bed were several symbols written in what appeared to be blood.

Grabbing the sheet from the floor beside her, Sarah began to scrub at the writing.

As each symbol was wiped away, her strength and thoughts grew clearer.

***

Sitting at Virginia McCleary's desk, Mark stared at the wall. Part of him wished he'd never came to South Carolina. He closed his eyes trying to push the vision of the snake biting Sarah from his mind. But when he did, he saw Rebecca there staring back at him. 'She couldn't have been there,' he thought to himself. He had to have imagined it. But why? Another wave of guilt washed over him.

"Damn it," he cursed, picking up the diary. "At least I can get some work done," he told himself. As he opened the book, the photo of Becca fell onto the desk.

He picked up the photo and examined it. His eyes focused on Becca's face and the crucifix necklace she was wearing. "God damn it," he grumbled.

A knock on the door startled him.

Catching his breath, he opened the door.

In front of him was Rebecca, wearing the same necklace.

"Mark, I just wanted to talk to you."

"I don't think it's a good time, Rebecca"

"Just hear me out. Please."

He sighed. "What is it?" he asked as he stepped into the hallway to talk to her. He shouldn't—couldn't—have her in his room.

"I feel really bad about what happened between us the other day. It really has been a crazy few weeks and if I have to tell the truth, I did have a bit of a crush

144

on you and did flirt a bit. I know it was completely inappropriate and disrespectful to your fiancée."

"It's okay." He didn't have the energy to argue about it.

"No, it's important," continued Rebecca. "I do like to play around a lot and may have caused problems with you and Sarah. I'm really sorry, especially after all the help you've given me."

"I appreciate that," he replied. He couldn't ask her about what had happened when Sarah was bitten. He had to have been mistaken.

"Can I give you a hug?" she asked. "No flirting. Just a hug."

"Sure," he replied.

***

Sarah, her balance slowly returning, walked to the door of her room. "Fucking bitches," she huffed. She would make Mark listen and if he cared about her at all, they would leave immediately.

She opened the door and stepped into the hallway.

Sarah looked up to see Mark and Rebecca sharing an embrace with Mark's back to her.

Rebecca's head was resting on Mark's shoulder, but she raised up and kissed him on the cheek. Then her gaze fell upon Sarah.

A triumphant smile came to Rebecca's face.

A combination of rage and heartbreak washed over her as she started toward them.

Rebecca's eyes were black, the smile still on her face.

Suddenly, the rage that swelled within her was overcome by the heartbreaking sense of loss. She'd lost him. She knew it.

She felt it.

Sarah closed her eyes momentarily and turned to go back into her room. As the door closed, she slid down the door onto the floor. Tears began to flow down her cheeks as she looked up toward the ceiling. "No. No. No," she repeated, beginning to sob.

After a few moments, the weight of loss began to lift, like a fog giving way to the light as Rebecca's influence waned.

"Fucking witch," grumbled Sarah, pulling herself to her feet. It was time to confront her, the only way Sarah knew how. Quickly moving to the closet, she pulled off her sweat soaked shirt and replaced it with a black 'ARMY' t-shirt. She then stepped out of her shorts and into a pair of jeans. As she pulled on her shoes, her mind raced through the list of objects she had seen in the house that would make a good weapon.

A splash from outside her window drew her attention and she looked outside.

Several figures gathered at the dock by the edge of the swamp. Soon they came into focus as her eyes adjusted to the darkness outside. She recognized Brianna, Clara, and Carson as they stood by two boats tied to the dock. The security guard, Miller, was standing in one of the boats. As she continued to watch, Rebecca joined them.

Once Rebecca arrived, they all entered the boat with Miller and pushed off from the dock.

"What the fuck?" she asked herself, watching the boat disappear into the darkness.

Sarah left her room and made her way down the hall. Something was going on. Something dark and she needed proof to show … "Asshole," she mouthed to herself as she passed the door to Mark's room. She thought about knocking in the door and just dragging him off but now she wanted proof. And possibly blood.

Quietly skulking down the stairs, she stopped at the kitchen. "This will have to do," she said to herself, grabbing a small knife from the counter. Wrapping the knife with a dish cloth, she slid it into her pocket before exiting the dimly lit house into the dark night.

Reaching the dock, Sarah scanned the darkness for signs of the boat carrying Rebecca and the others. There was nothing but the black of the night and the sounds of the swamp.

With a grunt of determination, she stepped into the second boat and untied it from the dock.

***

Sarah kept her body tucked in close to the deck as the boat drifted ashore. Slowing stepping into the muck, she scanned the area.

She saw flickering lights in the distance.

She began to creep forward, slowly feeling her way through the damp swamp with each step. Her body was taught and her senses were peaked. She'd done this before, but armed with an M4 instead of a kitchen knife.

After a few moments she stopped, taking cover by a large fallen tree. From her vantage point she saw several small fires illuminating a clearing in the swamp.

In the center of the fires a calf, tied to a stake, bellowed. As Sarah looked on, Rebecca, Brianna, Clara, and Carson stepped in the opening.

"What the …?" she mouthed.

Sarah heard garbled voices as she watched them walk in a circle around the calf. As they circled, the voices grew clear but not understandable as they unified into a chant. The volume increased but she still couldn't make out what they were saying. It seemed as if only every fourth or fifth word was English.

As Sarah concentrated on making out what they were chanting, she noticed Brianna step out of the circle and move toward the calf. The reflection of a knife flashed in the darkness as Brianna drove the blade into the calf's neck.

"Fuck," whispered Sarah.

The chanting quickened as Brianna held out a wooden cup to collect the blood.

"Fucking witches?" mouthed Sarah as his heart began to race and a chill washed over her body.

Brianna handed the cup to Rebecca.

Sarah put her hand to her mouth in disgust as Rebecca gulped down the blood, leaving trails pouring down her chin.

What had Mark—?

A branch snapped behind her and she spun around just as the butt of a rifled crashed into her head.

***

Sarah let out a moan as she slowly regained consciousness. Feeling the cold, damp ground, she looked up to see Rebecca and Miller standing above her.

"Sorry, kid," replied Miller. "You should've left."

"You just don't know when to mind your own business," said Rebecca, her chin and lips covered in the calf's blood.

"You're fucking witches?"

Miller reached down and grabbed Sarah by her shirt, pulling her to her feet. As he did, Rebecca spoke.

"Oh, sweetie. We're so much more than that …"

***

McCleary Plantation: February 15, 1865

As the sergeant buttoned his pants, Becca lay motionless on the couch behind him. She couldn't move. The pain—emotional and physical—was too much.

Curled into a ball on the couch, Becca slowly focused on the entrance to the room, where she saw Clara's mother rush into the hallway.

Seeing Henry's body, Clara's mother let out a scream.

"What's all that yellin' for? You ain't got a master no more," said the sergeant. "You're free!" he laughed.

"Where's my babies?" cried Clara's mother.

"They've been liberated too," laughed the sergeant as he shoved the distraught mother to the floor. "They're enjoyin' their day of jubilee in the swamp."

Clara's mother raised her head and let out wail only to receive a slap from the sergeant.

"Them darkies are floatin' in the swamp," said one of the other soldiers as they entered the room.

"Alright then," replied the sergeant. "On to the next Reb plantation, boys." He looked back toward Becca who'd pulled her knees to her chest trying to make herself even smaller. "But I doubt they'll bear as sweet a fruit as this one," he said with a smile.

Becca looked up toward the sergeant. Her pain began to shift to hatred—hot burning, all-consuming hatred. Behind the sergeant she saw Clara's mother rise to her feet and rush toward the door leading to the swamp.

The soldiers laughed as the distraught mother

ran to find her dead children.

"Let's go, boys," said the sergeant.

As the two soldiers exited the house, the sergeant turned toward Becca and smiled. "Bye, my little peach."

As the sound of muddy hooves and rattling metal faded away, Becca slowly rose to her feet and began to walk toward the back of the house. Oblivious to the cold sting of the rain, each step transformed more of her pain into anger. It did not take long to find Clara's mother, using her heartbroken wailing as a beacon.

Becca stopped behind the mother as she cried out for her children.

"Clara! Carson!" yelled the mother. "Where are my babies?"

Becca looked at the grief-stricken mother, but she was devoid of any emotion other than hatred.

"My babies," cried the mother.

"They killed Carson," said Becca flatly. "And Clara … she's dead too."

Clara's mother fell to her knees, wailing.

"They need to die," said Becca, turning back toward the house where the atrocities had occurred.

Clara's mother looked up toward Becca. Her grief replaced by something else as well.

As Becca looked on, the slave's brown eyes grew black, the darkness expanding from her pupils until her eyes were entirely black. "Do you want vengeance, Miss Becca?"

"I want them to die."

Clara's mother turned back toward the swamp and began to chant.

Lightning flashed over the swamp.

She continued to chant.

Another flash of lightning illuminated the dark swamp water.

It was bubbling like black tar over a fire.

"Come forth!" shouted Clara's mother.

As Becca looked on, a dark figure emerged from the swamp. Covered in mud and debris, it slowly waded out of the swamp and stopped in front of Clara's mother. Beneath the muck, Becca made out what looked to be small, black scales for skin. And its eyes—they burned red like a branding iron ready for use.

"Who calls upon me?" hissed the creature.

"We call for you, dark one," answered Clara's mother.

"And what is your desire?"

"Revenge," answered Becca.

The creature extended its hand and touched the mother's cheek. She grimaced as the skin began to *sizzle* where the creature touched her. "Do you want your children back, Priestess?"

"Yes. And this one wants revenge."

"I must have blood," said the creature, pointing toward Becca.

"It needs your blood, Miss Becca. And you must give it freely."

Becca shifted her gaze toward the creature as it walked to her and extended its dark, bone-thin hand.

"Blood," it demanded.

Becca leaned forward, spitting blood from her injured mouth into the creature's hand.

The creature closed its hand, hissing in satisfaction. "So much hate …good. You have been wronged girl. What is it that you desire?"

"I want them to die in agony," said Becca.

"And they shall," replied the creature before it

turned toward Clara's mother.

"And you, Priestess? What is your desire? You must say it."

"I want my children to live."

"Do you know what I will need?" asked the creature.

"I do," replied the woman, opening her arms wide. "And I give it freely."

Becca stood motionless, unmoved, as the creature drove its hand into the woman's torso and ripped her heart from her chest.

As Clara's mother fell to the ground, the creature turned back toward the swamp. Holding the heart above the water, it allowed the blood to trickle into the swamp.

Bubbles began to form and spread from where the blood hit the water. Soon the entire surface of the swamp was a bubbling cauldron.

A smile came to Becca's face as she saw Clara and Carson slowly rise from the murky water.

Lumbering out of the water, they stopped in front of Becca.

"They live and will do so forever, but they are tied to you and your offspring. What shall you have them do?"

"Kill them. All of them. And make them suffer."

"Yes, Miss Becca," answered Clara and Carson in unison as they walked past her to find the Union soldiers.

"Now for you girl," said the creature. "You have given your blood for this act, so you and your offspring must serve me.

"I don't care," replied Becca. "As long as they pay for what they did." She paused. "And this land remains with my family forever."

Becca let out a groan as the creature pulled her close. The smell of mud and sulfur filled her senses as she stared into its burning scarlet eyes.

"Your family shall keep this land," he said. "But you must mix your blood with that of your enemy," warned the creature. "Your hatred and their lust will combine to bring forth each generation of your family. You and your offspring must do this before your 25th year or you will lose this land forever. Once your blood has joined your enemies—"

"They die," said Becca.

"So it will be," laughed the creature.

Chapter Eleven

"Mark," said Sarah. "You need him."

"That's right. He's just another rich Yankee that will give the swamp his blood. And me his seed." Rebecca inhaled deeply and smiled. "Maybe our daughter will marry a President."

"Fuck you," cursed Sarah.

Sarah's head snapped to one side as Rebecca brought her open hand against her cheek.

"I want to have you tied up in the swamp so the snakes and gators can have you," grumbled Rebecca. "But you're such a pain in my ass, you'd probably get away," she continued before turning toward Clara and Miller. "You two take this Yankee bitch back down to the swamp and put a bullet in her brain." She stepped in close to Sarah. "Let the swamp have some more Yankee blood."

"Gladly, Miss Becca," replied Clara, grabbing Sarah and pulling her to her feet.

As Clara jerked her to her feet, Sarah grabbed the knife from her pocket and, with an animalistic grunt, drove it into Clara's neck just above the collarbone.

Clara shoved Sarah to the ground as she stumbled backwards and Miller leveled his weapon.

"Wait!" shouted Clara, regaining her balance and standing over Sarah. "You really have no idea what you're dealing with, do you Yankee filth?" asked Clara as she pulled the knife from her body and tossed it into the darkness.

Sarah looked up from the ground. Other than a small trickle of heavy black fluid, the wound was dry. She knew she'd hit her mark; this wasn't her first time driving a knife into flesh. Blood should have been pumping from Clara's body like a fountain. "What are you?"

Clara snatched Sarah off the ground, lifting her feet off the ground. "I've been with the McCleary family for a *very* long time," she said with a smile. "And you won't be the first Yankee soldier I've watched die."

Sarah turned back toward Rebecca, who smiled at her.

"Clara might actually hate you more than I do," said Rebecca. "See, it was fucking Yankee soldiers that killed her brother and then raped and killed her that night in 1865."

Sarah's mouth gaped. "No. It's not …" She paused, her attention still drawn to the wound that should have been a gusher.

Rebecca laughed. "You know, Miller. Why don't you let Clara rip her skin off before you shoot her?"

"You're the boss, ma'am," replied Miller, stepping close to Sarah, only inches away from her face. "I'm sure you wondered what it felt like when you were filleting some hajji bitch to get her to talk," he said to Sarah.

Sarah spat a mixture of blood and saliva onto Miller's face. "Fuck you," she cursed. "If I—"

The air left her lungs and Miller landed a blow to

her gut. Clara released her and she fell to the her knees. As she moved to push herself off the ground, another boot slammed into the side of her head.

Her head rang and vision clouded as she rolled onto her back, struggling to remain conscious.

"Enough!" shouted Rebecca. "Not here. Not on this ground."

Still dazed, Sarah felt herself lifted to her feet again. Through blurred vision, she saw Clara staring into her eyes. With a grunt, Clara tossed Sarah back to the ground like a rag doll.

"Take her," ordered Clara to Miller.

Miller pulled Sarah to her feet and directed her to follow Clara as she walked into the darkness.

Her head slowly clearing as she was led away, Sarah turned toward Miller. "How can you do this?"

"Sorry," replied the mercenary. "But it's just business. And Mrs. Mackey pays better than any shit-hole drug lord I've ever worked for." He gave her jerk and smiled. "And besides, I'm a Georgia boy and never really liked Yankees anyway."

"Stop talking to it," warned Clara. "Just get it to the water and we'll kill it."

Miller continued to prod Sarah as they walked back toward the edge of the swamp. Although her senses had returned following the blow to the head, she still purposely stumbled every few steps.

"I think this is good enough," declared Miller, stopping where Sarah had left her boat.

Clara stepped in front of Sarah. "I'd like to make you feel like I did that night," she said calmly as a chill ran down Sarah's spine. "To be beaten, then ..." She paused, her gaze still locked on Sarah. "... penetrated and shot like an animal."

"I didn't do—"

A powerful blow from Clara's open hand stunned her. "They thought they'd killed me with the bullet …" Clara grabbed Sarah's jaw, forcing her to look directly into her eyes. "…but I was still alive when they threw me in the swamp … to drown." A tear ran down Clara's cheek as she continued. "My whole body bruised and bleeding while I choked on the muddy, stagnant water."

"Ma'am," said Miller. "You can do whatever you want to her … but you should get to it."

Clara eyes burned through Sarah.

Clara suddenly turned to Miller. "Just take her to the edge and put a bullet in her brain."

Sarah had to act, or she would die.

"Let's go," said Miller, giving Sarah a shove.

Using the momentum of the shove, Sarah fell to the ground and swept Miller's legs, driving him to the ground with her. He grabbed for her arm, but she slammed her forehead into his nose and snatched the pistol from his vest.

"No!" shouted Miller as she pressed the barrel to his forehead and fired.

Pivoting to her left she fired two rounds into Clara as she lunged toward her.

Clara twisted away from her and fell to the ground but slowly began to rise to her feet again.

"Shit," cursed Sarah as she moved toward Clara, firing round after round into her until she fell backwards again.

Clara pushed herself out of the mud, but Sarah slammed her foot onto Clara's chest and drove her back onto the ground. Looking down the barrel, she centered on Clara's forehead and fired.

"Jesus," said Sarah as she grabbed the M4 from Miller's body and jumped into boat.

She pushed the boat away from the shore and began to pull at the starting cord for the motor when she heard noise and looked up to see Clara wading into the swamp. "Fucking die!" she yelled as she fired three bursts into Clara's chest.

Letting the M4 hang from its strap, she gave the cord another yank and the motor sputtered and came to life.

Reaching back to grab the rudder control she saw a hand come out of the water and then another as Clara grabbed the side of the boat and pulled her torso up to the side.

As Clara looked up, Sarah pressed the barrel of the M4 against her forehead and fired another burst.

Clara's head snapped backwards and she released her grip on the boat as it picked up speed.

Sarah collapsed onto the deck of the boat, panting. "Mark," she said out loud. She had to get to him. She twisted the throttle and aimed the boat for the McCleary House.

Racing over the water, Sarah focused on the dim reflection of moonlight on the murky water. Her mind race as she tried to make sense of everything that she had just heard and seen.

The weak, flickering specks of light from the main house came into view. As soon as she hit the dock, they were leaving, even if she had to knock him out and drag his ass away.

Sarah's body felt weightless as the boat slammed into a hidden obstacle in the water, sending her flying into the swamp.

Surfacing, she let out a groan and rolled onto her back as pain radiated from her leg. A flash of moonlight shown on a large piece of wood protruding from her left leg.

"Shit," she grumbled, looking back over her head to see the house now in view.

Grimacing, Sarah rolled onto her stomach and began to swim. Pushing the pain from her mind, she plowed through the water until she reached the shallows.

Standing, she grabbed the branch and yanked it from her leg. Pain shot through her body and she fell to her knees again.

The cold mud pulled at her arms and legs and the methane smell burned her nostrils as her breathing quickened. "Move, Captain," she ordered herself as she rose to her feet and began hobbling toward the house.

Grunting over the chirping of crickets and the croaking of frogs, she limped her way to the edge of the swamp.

At the edge, Sarah looked up to the house.

She could see Mark through the second-story window. He was sitting at his desk reading.

"Mark!" she yelled as she pushed herself forward. She glanced from her view of Mark to the swamp. Ten more feet. She looked up again and yelled. "Mar—"

Sarah's body arched backwards as pain exploded from her back. She felt herself pulled backwards into the arms of someone.

Another explosion of pain shot through her as a knife sank into her back for the second time.

Unable to resist, she felt her body spun around.

The midnight-black eyes of Rebecca met her gaze.

Rebecca grabbed Sarah's face and twisted it toward Mark's window, then back into her gaze.

***

"Mine," growled Rebecca as slid the blade across Sarah's throat. "Northern trash," she snarled, bathing in the warm splash of Sarah's blood as it splattered and spurted onto her face.

Rebecca raised her head toward the night sky and licked her blood-splattered lips. "See, Mother ..." she said to herself as she gave Sarah's lifeless body a shove, sending it crashing into the swamp. "... simple."

As she looked down at Sarah's body, two black hands emerged from the murky water. Sliding over Sarah's body, they pulled her downward until she disappeared.

Rebecca kept her gaze fixed on the water as two glowing red eyes came into view just under the surface. "Your will be done," she said and the eyes descended back into the black.

She looked up toward Mark's room and smiled.

***

Rebecca walked into the kitchen, still covered in Sarah's blood. Entering the room, she saw Bessy and Bailey sitting at the table.

They were waiting for her.

"It's done," declared Rebecca, tossing the blade on the table. "He will be easy to snare now."

"I suspect he will," said Bailey. "But that is not why we are here."

"No disrespect," said Rebecca, "but I—"

"Sit down," came a calm, powerful voice from behind Rebecca, causing her to sit.

She turned to see her mother, Brianna.

"What is this about?" asked Rebecca. "I did what I needed to do."

"Yes, daughter. You did exactly what you needed to," replied Brianna. "And that is why we are all here."

Looking over her mother's shoulder, she saw Carson and Clara, without a scratch from her run-in with Sarah, step inside and take up a position at each side of the door.

Rebecca's blood grew hot. "Tell me what this is about."

"Of course," said Bailey.

***

McCleary Plantation, Midnight, October 31st, 1868

Becca McCleary stood at the edge of the swamp. She ran her hand over the bump in her stomach and looked back toward the water. "It is done," she said.

The water began to bubble and the creature emerged from the depth and approached her.

"Why have you summoned me?" it hissed.

"I want more," replied Becca.

The creature burst from the water and was inches from Becca's face in a flash.

The smell of sulfur burned her nostrils, but she stood her ground.

"More?" asked the creature as it looked down upon her. "What more could you want?"

Becca's jaw tightened. "One dead Yankee per generation is not enough," she said. "I want them *all* to suffer."

The creature shifted its head from the left of Becca to the right, sniffing. "And by all of them?"

"All of them. I want the fathers burned, the son's torn apart by wild beasts, and the women taken …" She paused recalling the stench and pain of the sergeant from that night. "… over and over again by angry mobs before they watch their infants thrown to wolves."

A slow guttural laugh grew from the beast until it was a dull roar that Becca could feel in her bones.

"Very well, little witch," it replied. "But that will require more."

"Anything," declared Becca. "As long as I get to see it."

***

"So you see, young Rebecca," continued Bessy, "our dear Becca understood what it would take to truly make the Yankees suffer for what they did to our family."

Rebecca's pulse quickened as she stood. "I don't understand."

"Of course not," snapped Brianna. "Always so impetuous. So rash. All you wanted was the power. You never took time to respect what that power was meant for."

"That's not true. I've only done what the family has asked of me," she replied, taking a step away from the others.

"What Becca McCleary asked for so long ago will soon come to pass," said Bailey.

"What?" Rebecca's confusion began to mount. "What will come to pass?"

Now all three women were standing as Brianna continued. "The next offspring of this family will be male."

"No. That's not what—"

"And that man will reach the pinnacle of power," added Bessy. "And from this position, he will bring about a second Civil War. One in which the North and their liberal West Coast cousins will be consumed in the fires of chaos and destruction."

"No," declared Rebecca, shaking her head in disbelief. Looking into her mother's eyes, however, she knew it was true. "But we would be destroyed too. We can't—"

"As long as the North burns, nothing else matters," replied Bailey. "Nothing."

"But two things need to happen for the spell to be complete," said Brianna. "First, the swamp needed more Yankee again—which you provided."

"And what else?" asked Rebecca. "I will do whatever is needed."

"Our master needs McCleary blood to flow again so that the true matriarch may give birth to our instrument of destruction," said Brianna with a smile as she looked over Rebecca's shoulder.

"What are—" Rebecca turned toward the door.

Her blood turned to ice.

Shuffling through the door was a ragged, desiccated corpse in a shredded yellow dress.

"Mother! No!" screamed Rebecca, backing away from the thing moving toward her. "I am supposed to rule this family!" Summoning her rage, she called upon the creature for his power.

But none came, all that remained was fear. "Carson?" she pleaded, turning toward the family protector.

"Say hello to your ancestor and true leader of this family, Becca McCleary," declared Carson, his voice echoing through the room.

"You must do it, child," said Bailey. "Your blood for hers."

Rebecca turned to face the other women. Their eyes were black and their gaze locked on the ghastly creature slowly moving toward her. "No!" she pleaded as she turned to run. "I won't—"

She struggled for air as the corpse's hand wrapped around her neck.

"Mine," groaned the creature as it leaned forward, placing its dry, cracked lips over Rebecca's mouth.

Terror consumed Rebecca as she struggled to free herself from the creature's grip. She tried to scream as she felt her energy—her soul—fading.

***

Brianna and the others looked on as a black haze hovered over and around Rebecca and the corpse, eventually consuming them.

Then it began to fade.

Where Rebecca stood was a shriveled body lying on the floor, devoid of anything except skin and bones.

"Thank you, child," came a sweet, soft voice from where the corpse has stood.

In its place was a beautiful blonde woman with the deepest blue eyes in a restored bright yellow dress.

"It worked," declared Brianna, a tear of joy rolling down her cheek.

Becca McCleary bent over the remains of Rebecca and gently pulled the crucifix from the decayed body. "You're sacrifice has made this possible."

Becca then turned toward the other women. "I am pleased to see you have done so well for this family in my absence," she said with a smile. "My dear little Bailey," she continued as she walked over to the oldest of the women, placing a hand on her cheek. "I remember holding you in my arms so long ago."

She then turned toward Clara and Carson.

"And most of all, you two must be thanked," she said as they bowed their heads. "Your mother was the spark that set all of this in motion and you have kept the fire burning all these many years."

"It has all been for you, Becca," said Briana.

"Then we must get to work," replied Becca with a smile, draping the necklace around her neck.

***

Mark opened the door to an empty room. His brow furrowed as concern welled up inside him.

Where could she be? She couldn't walk yesterday and now … she's gone?

On the nightstand he saw a note. He moved closer but stopped.

His heart sank when he saw a ring setting on the note.

Mark stood motionless, the sound of his breath as loud as a jackhammer.

After a few long seconds, he slid the ring off the note onto the table and took the note in his hand.

He didn't want to read it. But he had to:

I'm sorry. It's just too hard right now. I need some time. You stay here and we will talk at the end of summer.

Please don't try to contact me before then. If you care, you will give me my space to figure this out.

Mark let the paper fall to the floor and collapsed onto the bed. He slowly raised his head, his gaze fixated on the ring setting on the nightstand.

"Is everything okay?"

He turned to see the resurrected Becca McCleary. Identical in appearance to Rebecca, he only saw the woman he had come to know over the last few weeks.

"She's—"

"I know," interrupted Becca. "Thomas said she asked him to take her to the airport in the middle of the night. She must have started feeling better and …

I don't know what to say."

"She's gone."

"Aren't you going after her?"

"She doesn't want me to," he replied, letting out a frustrated laugh. "She needs … time."

Becca sat next to him, putting her arms around him. "I'm sorry. I guess you'll be leaving now."

Mark stared at the floor. His pain slowly began to shift to frustration. And then anger. Why didn't she talk to him? He was only a few feet away and she just left.

He shifted his gaze toward Becca. There was something different about her but he couldn't pinpoint what it was. He didn't think it was possible, but her eyes were even more blue than the last time he'd seen her. "No. I want to finish my work. I need to."

"Well, I'm glad you're staying," she said with a smile before leaning in and giving him a quick kiss on his cheek. "I'll be here if you need me."

Epilogue

Mark stood at the podium overlooking a flag-covered casket. He looked up toward the grey, overcast sky and closed his eyes, summing his strength. Exhaling, he glanced down at the laminated notes in front of him.

The slight mist of rain formed small drops and trails on the notes. He wiped his hands over the laminated paper and looked up. He took another deep breath as his gaze fell on the flag draping over the casket.

Clearing his throat, he spoke.

"Today is a difficult day for me. For all of us." He took another breath, settling himself. "My loss is our loss. In this difficult time, I, like all of us, must turn to our families …" he paused looking to his left and giving a somber smile. "… and remember not my father's last days but his lifetime of works."

He looked toward the casket once more and stepped down from the podium and slowly took his seat. He placed his hands on his knees but they wouldn't stop shaking.

A hand rested on his.

He looked up, pausing briefly on the crucifix necklace before looking into Becca's eyes.

"I'm here for you," she said softly.

***

Becca turned back toward casket, her stomach churning with hatred as she looked at the American flag but content in the death of another Northern man.

The crack of rifles firing the salute caused Mark to jump and she squeezed his hand slightly.

Another volley echoed across the cemetery.

She glanced toward him as a tear trickled down his cheek.

The final volley fired as a smile came Becca McCleary's face.

Other Works by Brian Dorsey

Gateway Military Science Fiction Series
Gateway (Gateway Book 1)
Cold Planet (A Gateway Universe Story)
Saint (Gateway Book 2)
Saint (Gateway Book 3)
Rise of the Wolf: Katalya's Story (A Gateway
Universe Novella)
Schism (Gateway Book 4)

Comic Book Series
The Book of Luka
The Book of Jessica
War Angels